Having spent many years working in the family business, Kate got the opportunity to fulfil a dream of sitting down and writing when she took early retirement. As a busy mother and lately grandmother, her family has always been central to her days and so, it was natural that her first novel would revolve around family dynamics. Her children Adam and Francesca, are now grown but she blends her writing days with being Nanna to Connor and Evie, living in Kent with husband Keith and mad Labrador Jaffa.

For Cecilia—always loved, always missed.

To/
Joy and Keith

Enjoy!

Kate x

Kate Merrin

THE TIES THAT BIND

AUSTIN MACAULEY PUBLISHERS™

LONDON • CAMBRIDGE • NEW YORK • SHARJAH

A CIP catalogue record for this title is available from the British Library.

ISBN 9781035806478 (Paperback)
ISBN 9781035806973 (ePub e-book)

www.austinmacauley.com

First Published 2023
Austin Macauley Publishers Ltd®
1 Canada Square
Canary Wharf
London
E14 5AA

Huge thanks to Ches and Mandy for their help in reading and re-reading the manuscripts and to Louise for the laughs, tears, wine and takeaways. Most especially, endless thanks to Keith for his support, letting me shut myself away to scribble at odd times of the day and night, and believing that those scribbles would get into printed form.

Table of Contents

Chapter 1

The phone rang. Vanessa hadn't long been at her desk in her home office, but looking at the screen, the caller ID showed it was her sister Diana. Given the events of the last few days, she wasn't surprised to get the call, though from Diana's tone, it was obvious something was wrong.

"Mummy's collapsed. It looks like a stroke. Edith called in and found her slumped in bed. The ambulance is on its way."

Edith was their mother's neighbour. Neither Vanessa nor Diana were particularly taken with her, both feeling there was a greater degree of nosiness than actual compassion eliciting from her regular drop-ins to their parents' home. However, she had her uses, including popping in to check that their mother, Edwina, was ok. This is what had happened today.

Edwina at 91 was a widow of over 20 years; stoical, independent and quite Edwardian in her outlook. But in the last few days, she'd struggled with her health and had given in and agreed the GP should be called. Urine and blood tests were in the pipeline and both her daughters had spent the day before organising some simple suppers, providing nourishing drinks and generally ensuring that Edwina could ride out this current storm and be back on her feet in the coming days.

Diana had been due at the bungalow where Edwina had lived for over 40 years around 10 am but they'd asked Edith if she could pop in early to give their mother a cuppa and some toast. She had found her slumped half out of bed, slurring her speech, confused and fretful.

"Ok, I'm on my way." Vanessa immediately went into practical mode. Her husband, Daniel, sitting across the desk from her mouthed, "what's up?" She flapped her hand at him. It looked an irritated gesture, but it genuinely wasn't. She was trying to gather her thoughts.

As the youngest sister, Vanessa often deferred to Diana. She had, however, spent 20 years working in the health service and so, for anything medically related, they switched roles, and she tended to be the calm one who understood the terminology and the systems.

Diana sounded calm, but panicky—an oxymoron if ever there was one. She liked to be in control and be planned to the nth degree, so this sudden turn of events challenged her sense of order.

"Are they taking her to Eastbourne or Brighton?" Vanessa enquired.

"No idea, I'll find out and phone you. Drive safely, see you soon."

Vanessa put the phone down and looked at Dan who was waiting to hear the details of the call.

"Looks like Mummy's had a stroke. The ambulance is on its way. Edith found her this morning. No idea how long she was like it. I'm going to the hospital and Diana will meet me there." As she rattled off the information, she was gathering her things together.

Simba, their Fox Red Labrador, who spent his days under her desk, looked up hopefully.

It didn't look like a potential walk situation but you could never be too sure. "I'll drive you."

"No it's fine, you stay here, man the fort."

"I'll drive you," Dan said again, giving her a determined stare that translated to 'don't argue.'

"Ok, thanks. I'll just pop to the loo. Diana will phone to say if it's Eastbourne or Brighton but we can head in the general direction."

Just then the phone rang again. 'Diana', announced the phone screen ID. "Hi."

"It's Eastbourne. They don't know if it is a stroke but I told them the GP is doing tests. They've said the hospital will know more. I'm going to lock up and follow the ambulance."

"Ok, see you there. Dan's driving me, so we'll be an hour or so. Take care."

"Eastbourne," Vanessa said to her husband.

They hustled Simba into his basket, set the house alarm and headed to the Sussex coast. As they pulled out of the driveway, Dan patted her leg.

"She'll be ok, I love you."

She smiled back at him, patted his hand back and often as she'd done before, offered up a silent thank you to the Gods for having this man beside her.

Chapter 2

They'd managed to find a parking space surprisingly easily for 10:30 on a Thursday morning. There was a general bustle in the main hospital entrance—wheelchairs, pushchairs, people on sticks and in plaster casts. Old, young, sick, new-borns and the dying—it felt like an ocean of humanity to swim through as they dodged and weaved their way towards the A&E signs.

Vanessa walked purposefully holding Dan's hand. The familiar smell of the hospital enveloped her. She had spent four happy years working in the Urology and Colorectal Department of a London Teaching Hospital when she had qualified aged 18 before working in Harley Street and a variety of GP surgeries. Everyone assumed she was a nurse when they heard she worked for the NHS. Interestingly, no one ever thought she'd been a doctor! Vanessa though wasn't one to take offence at such blatant sexism. She had loved her job as a medical secretary. Working with talented surgeons, immersed in the drama of the sick but without the demands placed on those skilled hands who, sometimes literally, were responsible for life and death decisions. Even now, over 30 years later, there was a sense of homecoming as she walked into a hospital environment.

Diana was perched on a plastic chair at the end of the row in the corridor.

Observing her from a distance, Vanessa saw her eyes darting backwards and forwards, taking in all the movements and conversations around her. She fiddled distractedly with the handle of her handbag. Glancing around, her eyes alighted on her young sister and Dan and her face broke into a smile.

They hugged tightly, Diana leaning into Dan who enveloped her in a hug. He was a tall, well build man in his late 50s. He'd known Diana and her husband Mike longer than he'd known Vanessa. He'd been best man at their wedding which is where he'd met Vanessa. She was five years younger than Diana and they'd always had a good relationship. Diana liked to be organised and methodical; Vanessa was happy for the majority of the time to allow her older sibling to take the lead. Only occasionally, when Vanessa felt particularly strongly about something, would she disagree with her sister. She disliked confrontation—a lot— and would prefer to bite her tongue than cause a row. It was a balance that suited them both and worked well.

There was a much older sister—Jennifer. Neither had spoken to her for over 10 years. She was currently residing somewhere at Her Majesty's Pleasure—fraud charges that had rocked the whole family and broken Edwina's heart. Her absence suited Diana and Vanessa just fine.

"Any news?"

"No, I followed the ambulance and they're checking her in. They know we're here and said they'd come and get us."

Dan suggested he go and get some teas.

"I'll have a black coffee," Vanessa had said. She'd recently self-diagnosed that lactose was causing her some unpleasant stomach symptoms and so she'd cut out milk. She'd kill for a comforting milky latte right now but could do without becoming intimately acquainted with the A&E toilet facilities.

"Well, you're in the right place if you get the shits," Dan quipped. He was nervous in hospitals and generally uncomfortable around sickness.

Vanessa gave him a watery smile as if to say 'not now, eh.' He squeezed her shoulder and went off in the direction of the Costa Café.

Sitting alongside her sister, Diana recounted the same details she shared on the phone about how Edwina had been found.

"The paramedics were there when I got there. Edith was fussing around, sticking her beak in as if she was the one to talk to them. I told her thanks, I'd deal with it. She wasn't happy but I told her I'd update her when we had some news. God, she loves a drama."

"Well, at least she was there to get things moving by calling the ambulance. Do we know how long Mummy had been like it?"

"She said she was trying to get up to get to the bathroom, but frankly, she wasn't making much sense at all. Kept saying her shoulder hurt and that was the problem and why she couldn't get herself out of bed."

Edwina had complained for some months of a stiff shoulder and had taken to blaming it for all her current poor health.

"She screamed when they tried to move her," Diana said quietly, "it was awful."

Edwina, named after her father Edward, had always been a stoical force for her children. Generally, uncomplaining about her own advancing frailties she didn't hold with fussing about herself. 'I've a lot to be thankful for,' was her mantra. So, seeing her as a helpless old lady, brought low by sickness and pain was a new experience for the girls.

Dan appeared with three large polystyrene cups of tea and coffee. It was surprisingly drinkable but he'd informed them that it was a Costa concession in reception, so that explained it. He also mentioned they'd need to make it last because you needed a mortgage to afford any more.

"Oi, how long do we have to wait?" A woman in her 20s with a variety of piercings, Ugg boots and purple spiky hair accosted a nurse who had brought a sick bowl to a young chap sitting across from them in a wheelchair. The woman had a child of about two on her hip. A trail of green snot oozed from its nose, down onto a grubby Ninja turtle t-shirt. Denim shorts and greyish socks, though they'd obviously started life as white, completed the child's wardrobe. Given that it was a December day, Vanessa thought the child must be freezing. She couldn't help but look critically at the young woman and immediately felt guilty for doing so. No one knew what had brought them here—maybe her mother was dying in a cubicle too.

The nurse glowered. "We'll call you when the police have finished with him," she said loudly enough for the assembled crowd to enjoy the entertainment being enacted before them. Not a dying mother then!

Diana cast an eye at Vanessa and raised her eyebrow. They both knew the look meant 'charming, what a lovely family,' but neither looked at the young woman again for fear it might provoke her.

Dan was preoccupied with the chap in the wheelchair. He was studiously watching whether the sick bowl was going to be employed. A potential upchucking situation would be more than he could handle.

"Just going to check outside on the phone, see if any emails have come in." He carried his tea and exited through the double doors at a speed Usain Bolt would be proud of! Vanessa smiled. She knew he wasn't really wanting to be here, but wouldn't leave her until they had some answers.

Diana propelled herself out of the chair.

"I'm going to find out what's going on."

They went to the Welcome Desk window. In reality, there was nothing welcoming about the slightly mottled Perspex hole in the wall. It reminded Vanessa of a railway booking office in the old days when you had to bend down to shout through the little slit in order to be heard.

On the other side sat a rather well built individual whose badge announced her to be 'Rose.' Personally, Diana thought she had more of a look of a bulldog chewing a wasp, but she garnered her best smile and launched into her enquiry.

"I wonder if you can help. Our mother was brought in about an hour ago and we just wondered when we'd be able to see her?"

"Name," barked Bulldog Rose.

"Diana, Diana Williams."

The bulldog proceeded to type into her keyboard.

"I think she might have meant Mummy's name," murmured Vanessa. "Bollocks, sorry. Edwina, Edwina Thompson with an H and a P."

18

At that point, a nurse appeared in the doorway. To both Diana and Vanessa, she looked about 12 but with a kindly yet authoritative voice said, "We're just finishing taking her history. Sorry, it's been manic this morning and we had a backlog of ambulances. Take a seat and I'll come and find you."

"Thanks so much," they said in unison and smiled weakly at Bulldog Rose as they returned to the plastic chaired waiting area.

Dan reappeared. "Nothing's come in. I called Caitlin and asked her to drop in and feed Simba later. She's going to give him a run too."

Caitlin was their daughter. Recently married to Sam, she lived 10 minutes from her parents. Her wedding a couple of months ago was the last 'family do' they'd all been at and Edwina had thoroughly enjoyed herself. It was obvious though that she had been struggling through the day, with new faces and a changed routine. Ross, their eldest, worked in London and lived in Crystal Palace with his fiancée Charlotte. Both children were close to their 'nanna' and Vanessa was worried about Caitlin's reaction.

"I just said she was having some tests after the GP's visit earlier this week," said Dan. "I've not told Ross, best wait till we know what's happening."

"Why don't you head over to Michael? There's nothing you can do here and we may be some time. At least that way you can do some work and be comfy." Vanessa knew he wanted to support her but felt that for now she needed to not worry about him too. "Ok, if you're sure. Call us when you hear something."

"Will do and Diana can give me a lift back."

Dan put his arms around his wife and kissed the top of her head. "See you later, love you." Vanessa took a deep breath and absorbed the woody smell of aftershave and deodorant. It was familiar, comforting and always made her feel grounded.

"Love you, drive carefully."

Dan pecked his sister-in-law on the cheek and gave her a brief hug. He disappeared through the swing doors and Vanessa watched him go. Would she be an orphan when she saw him again?

They sat, not talking, but people watching and trying to be patient. After 20 minutes or so the 12-year-old nurse reappeared and beckoned to them. Taking up their coats and bags, the two sisters followed her beyond the Welcome Desk and into the hubbub of A&E.

They braced themselves for what they would face.

Chapter 3

Edwina was in pain. Everything hurt, every joint, every muscle, and a desperate burning pain 'down below.' She lay on the hospital trolley in her nightdress, a thin blanket covering her and her favourite red slippers flopping off her swollen feet.

She wanted to die.

People were fussing around her—clips on her fingers, beeping machines, blood pressure cuffs, temperature gauges poked in her ear, lights in her eyes. Why couldn't they all just go away and leave her be?

Edwina was an only child. Her father had died when she was just eighteen months old and she was brought up by her hard-working widowed mother and her adoring, but Victorian, grandparents. She'd married at twenty-three in 1947 to James, her first love who she'd met when she was thirteen. He was in the Navy and they'd had a happy and successful marriage for 45 years. Three daughters had produced several grandchildren and after several years of ill health, James succumbed to a poor heart and diabetes in 1992. Edwina was just 68. She felt cheated of their retirement. They had plans to spend their old age together, though in truth, James knew he'd never make old bones. She'd been a widow now for over twenty years. It seemed impossible. She talked to him every day and he had left her comfortably provided for, so she had been able to stay in their beloved home. A child of a frugal mother and careful grandparents, Edwina liked to buy things for her girls and their children, but was something of a scrooge when it came to her own expenditure. A small two-bar fire was perfectly satisfactory rather than running the central heating through the bungalow and she was known to carefully unwrap presents, saving the wrapping for birthdays and Christmas. A good iron and no one would know it was second hand. She liked to be 'band-box smart' when she met friends for lunch, but would happily garden in her old jumper with holes in the elbows, and if she could get away with darning her stockings she did.

She now lay on the trolley surrounded by the noises from the emergency department and she felt exhausted. She just wanted to sleep, and preferably not wake up. She'd been feeling low and miserable for weeks now and there was a disappointment that every day she realised she'd survived another night.

One of the nurses stuck her head round the curtain. "Are you ok, Edwina?"

Any other time, she would have been annoyed at some flibbertigibbet calling her by her first name. She had great grandchildren older than this girl, but weariness overcame her and she smiled weakly.

"Yes, thank you, dear."

"Your daughters are here to see you. Shall I show them in?"

This caused Edwina's eyes to widen. Her girls, her babies, they mustn't see her like this. They could visit when she was home later.

"No, no, it's fine. I'll see them later. Thank them for coming and I'll call when I'm home." Her reply was panicky, desperate for the nurse to understand that her daughters mustn't be exposed to this.

Gently, kindly, but firmly, the nurse replied, "Oh, but they're here now and they've been waiting ages. How about a quick hello, just so they know you're ok?" And with that, she disappeared on the other side of the curtain.

Edwina sighed. She hated not being in control. *So much for patient consent,* she thought. The curtain gently moved aside and Vanessa and Diana came in. They moved to either side of the bed and gently took one of Edwina's hands in theirs. The skin on them was dry, wrinkled and aged, but they were hands that had bathed them, dried their tears, comforted them over the years and never once been raised in anger. Edwina was proud that she had never smacked any of her children.

"Hello, you," they both said in unison, quietly and with a small smile playing on both their faces.

It was more than Edwina could bear. Tears trickled down her lined face and her voice wavered.

"Oh, darlings, I'm so sorry."

Both women stroked their mother's hands and gently wiped away her tears. "You've nothing to be sorry for."

"Everyone has been so kind, doctors, nurses, the ambulance men. I'm such a nuisance."

"You're just a bit poorly," Vanessa said. "That's what everyone is here for, to help you feel a bit better."

"It's your turn to be looked after for a while," Diana explained.

"You're such good girls." Edwina held onto her daughters' hands as she gently drifted off to sleep, safe in the cradle of their clutches.

Chapter 4

As the December light faded, Vanessa and Diana sat with a glass of wine in hand in Diana's sitting room. Dan and Michael had gone to get a Chinese takeaway and a call to Caitlin had sorted Simba for the night. He'd go and stay with them and be allowed to sleep on Caitlin and Sam's bed so at least one member of the family was enjoying today! Caitlin said she'd update Ross and Charlotte too, so that was another job sorted.

Vanessa absently stroked the head of Churchill, Diana and Michael's spaniel. He rolled onto his back presenting a fluffy white tum for attention. She smiled and obliged by giving him a tickle. Roosevelt, their other younger Springer looked offended from the other side of the room. He was missing out on the attention but frankly couldn't be arsed to move from the comfort of the armchair he'd commandeered.

"Let's hope they've found her a bed."

Diana took a sip of her Pinot Grigio. It was her tipple of choice though Vanessa preferred a G&T. However, just for now, alcohol in any form was needed so she was content with the large glass in her hand.

"She seemed a bit better with the catheter in, less anxious."

Vanessa sat silently stroking Churchill and musing over the events of the afternoon. Edwina had continually fretted she wanted to 'spend a penny' but the yells and screams that elicited from her whenever anyone tried to move her were pitiful. She'd sat propped on a commode for over an hour, leaning into Vanessa who propped her up and was desperately trying to keep her mother warm and with some semblance of dignity for the old lady. Edwina had been shaking with the effort of being upright and seemed to be flitting between consciousness and pure exhaustion for the duration of the time she'd sat, unable to pass anything. In the end, the staff had decided to put in a catheter. Vanessa and Diana had left the A&E staff to it whilst they'd got more tea and when they returned, Edwina claimed it was more comfortable. They couldn't help noticing though that she fretfully tugged at the tube and claimed it stung.

"You've probably got an infection and that's why it's stinging," said Vanessa. She tried easing her mother's hands away from the catheter tube. "Just relax and now you don't have to worry about getting up or wetting the bed."

Their mother had a morbid fear of wetting the bed. She claimed it went back to boarding school. As the child of a deceased Mason, Edwina was entitled to attend the Masonic School in South London in 1929 when she was aged just five. Fear and loneliness, not to mention confusion at no longer being with her beloved nanna and grandpa meant that on her first night, she had wet the thin mattress covering the iron bedstead in her dormitory. The housemistress, whose name had dispersed with the passing of time, had called her a 'dirty little bitch' and made Edwina strip and remake the bed. She'd been held up as a bad example to the other girls and the shame and disgrace had stayed with her for life. It never occurred to Edwina that her housemistress had been the bitch, behaving so cruelly to a five-year-old little girl. She had always remained convinced it was her punishment to endure and once again, it had reared its ugly head as she lay on the A&E trolley. Covered in a thin blanket, she shivered. She had on her dressing gown and slippers but the events of the morning meant that shock was starting to set in. Both girls took off their winter coats—Diana's was more of a walking jacket, but padded and she wrapped it round the shoulders of her mother. Vanessa had a black winter coat with soft fur collar and she draped it over Edwina making sure the collar acted as a muffler for her chilled shaking hands.

"Would you like a cup of tea, Mummy"?

"That'd be lovely, thank you, darling." Diana bustled off saying she'd try and find some biscuits too.

Vanessa rubbed her mother's hands.

"You want to watch out for her?" Edwina had whispered. "Who?"

"Diana likes to be in charge. She bosses everyone around. She's got a nasty streak in her."

Vanessa was taken aback. Everyone knew Diana liked to be in control—much like her mother—but they also knew it came from a place of kindness and wanting to be able to help.

Edwina was not given to voicing her thoughts so viciously or so loudly. It was out of character and Vanessa found her mother's comments upsetting.

"She's just very worried about you. She wants to make sure everything is being done for you. You know what she's like."

"Little Miss Bossy, don't you let her walk all over you."

"It's fine, I won't, don't worry. I'd be lost without her."

Vanessa had thought it best to change the subject and started chatting about Simba's latest antics, a topic that always amused and entertained her mother.

Now, several hours later in the fading light of Diana's home, she mulled over what her mother had said. Vanessa obviously hadn't said anything to Diana. She knew she would be heartbroken to think her mother had voiced such thoughts.

What was disturbing to Vanessa was it was so out of character for Edwina.

"I thought she was quite bolshy today. I guess that must be the infection. At least with the catheter in she should have a reasonable night."

"Mmm." Diana was distracted by her own thoughts.

"Do you think we ought to mention the Living Will?" Diana asked. Vanessa's head shot up. Their mother had made a living will several years before, content she didn't want to 'be a cabbage and a burden to you girls.' She had also sorted a Power of Attorney, a Health Power of Attorney, naming both girls as representatives, and had bought and paid for her funeral! She took great delight in telling people she was forward thinking and organised and religiously kept her Living Will in her handbag for safe keeping. Both girls had copies.

"I think it's a bit early to worry about that yet," Vanessa had said. "They're sure it wasn't a stroke and just a urine infection. A dose of antibiotics and she should be right as rain." Vanessa wasn't sure she wholly believed what she was saying. There was no doubt Edwina was very poorly and had been silently struggling for a while, but it seemed a bit callous to start considering a DNR just yet.

Do not resuscitate, she went over it in her mind. An acronym from her past that she might now have to face in her own family. So many abbreviations from her old career ambled around in her memory. There would have been a multitude of them used today—

FBC, CxR, KUB, U&Es, TATT, BP.

Edwina's chart was a kaleidoscope of terms and phrases that were a language all of their own but their cadence provided some comfort to Vanessa. They were terms she knew, understood and ultimately meant someone was doing something practical for her mother. "I suppose you're right," Diana said. "Let's see what they say tomorrow."

The men arrived back with plastic bags filled with chicken chowmein, sweet and sour pork, crispy chilli beef and prawn crackers. They'd agreed to eat together and then Dan was heading home. He had a couple of meetings the following day and he'd return on Saturday to collect Vanessa by which time everything should be clearer with a plan of action in place.

They ate the food though in reality, tasted very little and then Dan said his goodbyes and headed off. As he drove away, Diana, Vanessa and Michael cleared the kitchen, made a cup of tea and settled down to watch Masterchef on catchup. In truth, Vanessa's head was pounding. *Probably the bloody Pinot*, she thought.

Dan sent a WhatsApp message to say he was home and heading to bed. He'd sent a couple of heart emojis and a row of kisses.

"Do you mind if I grab a bath?" Vanessa had said. Her head was now home to a brass band and she fretted a migraine was going to start. "Help yourself, you know where everything is."

"Thanks, see you in the morning."

Vanessa headed up the stairs and ran a long, hot bubble bath. She soaked for 10 minutes with a facecloth over her eyes, steaming and waiting for the paracetamol she'd taken from the bathroom cabinet to kick in.

Not for the first time was she grateful that she and Diana treated each other's houses as their own. They knew where things were kept and Diana had put a cotton nightshirt on the bed for her sister to use. Vanessa climbed in, a spaniel on either side of her to keep her company and immediately turned out the light. She usually liked to read or check Facebook before settling down but she was wiped out and fell into an immediate, and surprisingly, dreamless sleep.

Chapter 5

They arrived at the hospital late morning. An early call had established that Edwina had been moved to Larch Ward and had had a reasonable night. Diana had been out and walked the dogs and during her absence Vanessa had taken a call from Edwina's GP.

"I just wanted to check on how she was doing following my visit on Monday—and I've got the blood and urine results back."

Vanessa updated Dr Logan on the events of the previous day and that they were due to go in this morning to see how she was.

"I'm so sorry, she was obviously pretty poorly on Monday. The urine sample shows she's got an infection but I expect the hospital will have found that and put her on antibiotics. However, her Vitamin D is also extremely low. That may account for some of her aches and pains and for a bit of her forgetfulness. Can you let the hospital know and they can provide some supplements for her? I'm happy to speak with them if you need me to."

Vanessa had thanked her and said she'd update the surgery when they had more news. "See about some care help for her," Dr Logan advised. "She certainly needs a bit of extra help till she's back on her feet and the hospital will be able to sort out community nursing. You'll need to push it though, they'll try and get you both to do it."

Vanessa put the phone down as Diana walked through the door. She updated her sister and they sat for a while in the lounge, dogs at their feet and coffee in hand.

"She won't like someone coming in," Diana said.

"She won't have a choice—we'll have to arrange things and it's only temporary. We can't both do it and she wouldn't take it from us anyway, you know what she's like."

It felt disloyal to be passing the care of their mother to the nurses but Vanessa was pragmatic enough to know that it could take some time for Edwina to regain her strength and both women had other responsibilities and couldn't practically be full time nurses. Edwina would resist strongly if she felt her girls were having to look after her.

Diana sighed, and rubbed her temples.

"I best update Edith," she said, picking up her mobile and dialling. Fortunately, it went to answerphone, so she left a brief message and said they'd be in touch when they knew more. She then dialled Sandra and Tony, Edwina's other neighbours. They were a retired couple but spritely with lots of hobbies and Tony often helped Edwina with little jobs around the house. Sandra was a stylish, polished lady with a heart of gold. Vanessa often thought of her as French—she had that classic look that she could be wearing jeans and a t-shirt but had an effortlessly elegant style. They were kind, thoughtful neighbours who held the emergency key for the bungalow. Both Sandra and Tony were cautious about Edith's apparent eagerness to be always on the scene though this was only something they'd shared with Diana in recent times when she was visiting Edwina at home and had hello'd across the driveway. They'd had a catch up and both Tony and Sandra had been anxious that Edwina was a bit out of sorts. How right they'd been.

Diana got through to Tony and let him have the latest news. Edith had been round to all the neighbours, so they were aware she had collapsed and he promised to keep an eye on the bungalow over the next few days.

They rinsed their coffee cups, settled the dogs, jumped into Diana's red Ka and headed to the hospital.

Edwina was sitting in a chair alongside her bed. She had on her dressing gown that was a relic of the 1980s—floral and quilted it was now about six inches too long for her, so trailed behind her like an unsightly wedding train. Her burgundy slippers were on her feet which were both a mottled shade of blue veins that come with age. Her once auburn curly hair was wispy and white, sticking up all over her head in tufts of down. Soft but flyaway. Good job she didn't have a mirror to hand or she would have been mortified. Her teeth were still in her bathroom at home. In the kerfuffle to get her into the ambulance, her dignity had taken second place and so, she was toothless which gave her mouth a somewhat pinched and sunken look.

At the end of the hospital bed was a plastic bag with some contents inside including her handbag—no teeth but she'd go nowhere without her handbag! Also inside was a hospital sanitary set which included some soap, a toothbrush—unused—and toothpaste, the small tube variety often handed out on long haul flights.

Her bed was by the window and the radiator blasted hot air into the humid room. The December day outside was bright but chilly, whereas inside the ward, it was positively tropical enough for some limbo dancing and cocktails. Her view looked out onto the dull grey patina of the opposite side of the hospital, row upon row of windows looking like the catacomb holes for burials that you see on an Italian hillside.

Edwina looked around her with suspicious, restless eyes. It was a mixed ward and there was a young chappy opposite with his leg raised in traction. He had jogging bottoms on but no shirt or top. Edwina tutted to herself—she felt exposed and uncomfortable in a room with strangers and some of them men at that. Next to traction man was an old boy, asleep, mouth agape and rumbling snores emanating from deep in his chest. Edwina thought that but for the noise he could pass for a corpse.

The bed next to him was empty and then immediately next to Edwina was another old lady. In truth, she was younger than Edwina but it was a failing of hers that she considered anyone over the age of seventy as old, whilst refusing to see herself as anything other than vibrant and active. She happily played the poor old widow woman when it suited her but in the main she felt she was 'with it' and barely middle aged.

She spied her daughters at the entrance to the ward, looking up and down either side, locating the familiar face of their mother.

Both were surprised to see her sitting up in the chair after her frail and despondent appearance of the day before. Edwina's deep brown eyes surveyed them as they approached. She was stuck in this place because of them.

Chapter 6

"Hello," Vanessa said, a smile on her face as she bent to kiss the papery dry cheek of her mother.

"You're looking better today."

"Good morning," Diana said, more formally but with a smile and relieved that her mother's distress of the previous day had passed.

"Did you sleep well?"

Edwina, who didn't take kindly to being patronised like a child raised her eyebrows heavenward.

"What, with that racket!" She indicated to Mr Snorer across the way.

"What with him and," she cocked her head to the left where the elderly lady in the next bed was humming, somewhat tunelessly, "we'll meet again."

"How are you feeling?" Vanessa noticed the catheter was no longer in place.

"Absolutely fine, lot of fuss about nothing."

At that moment, a large man in a pink checked shirt and open collar appeared. His sleeves were rolled up and he had an air of authority and entitlement around him.

"Good morning, Edwina," he muttered, picking up her chart from the end of the bed. He didn't make eye contact.

Edwina, recognising her opportunity to make a good impression and escape, smiled sweetly.

"Good morning, doctor." Her tone was deferential. He looked up. That God-like pedestal the older generation invariably placed around their doctors was in evidence here.

"Well, you've had a good night. All looks fine and we'll get you home today." He put the chart back as Edwina smiled, nodded and thanked him.

"Excuse me." Vanessa was irked that he hadn't had the good grace to even acknowledge their presence or for that matter bother to introduce himself.

"Her GP called this morning to say she has a urine infection and low Vitamin D. She also said that Mummy would need some community nursing when she goes home. Will that be sorted today before you discharge her?"

The consultant looked Vanessa up and down.

"Are you happy to go home?" He addressed Edwina directly. "Oh yes, absolutely."

"You don't need any help?"

"Absolutely not, I have lived on my own for many years, doctor. I'm fine by myself."

He looked at Vanessa.

"Well, your mother is happy so that is all that matters." With that, he turned away and approached the Vera Lynn tribute act in the next bed.

Raising her voice, Vanessa wasn't going to let this go.

"She was extremely poorly yesterday in A&E and there was some question as to whether she had been taking her medication." Edwina had been too confused to remember if her thyroid pills had been taken, or her eye drops.

"Evidently, she needs some support for now," Vanessa pushed on.

"No, all good to go. Goodbye, m'dear."

"Excellent," said Edwina, looking to stand up and get out asap.

"Hang on," Diana said. "At least let's find out if you need any antibiotics or anything."

Edwina sat back in her chair, looking bad tempered and belligerent.

"Well, you two needn't look so disappointed."

"Look, we just want to make sure you're safe and you've got what you need. Daddy would expect us to do that at least." Diana had adroitly played the trump card to employ their father's name into the conversation which was a guarantee to encourage Edwina to be reasonable.

"I'll go and find a nurse." Diana left the bedside, giving her sister a wink. "I'll grab a cuppa for everyone too."

Vanessa sat on her mother's bed and took her hand. "Dr Logan called today to see how you were."

"Dr Logan?"

"Yes, the GP who came to see you on Monday."

"Ah, yes." Edwina clearly didn't remember. She suddenly felt tired and worn out. Vanessa noticed the change in demeanour, like a balloon that deflates, her mother seemed to crumple and fold in on herself.

"Would you like to put your feet up for a bit?"

Edwina nodded and Vanessa helped her gently but firmly out of the chair. Having spent much of her teens helping their increasingly frail father from his chair to his bed, she was well used to the manoeuvre. A gentle hand behind her mother's neck and a grasp under her arm, helped Edwina to propel herself to her feet.

Edwina winced. Everything still hurt. She must be coming down with the flu.

Vanessa guided her a couple of steps to the bed and as gently as possible, lowered her.

Edwina hoped the young chap opposite didn't get an eyefull up her nightdress, but frankly, right now, she didn't care.

Vanessa arranged the pillows as her mother lay back, half sitting, half lying. They were thin and coarse. What was needed was some plump, soft duck down ones to encircle the shoulders and provide a downy rest for the head. But for now, a thin blanket and thin pillows were all that there was.

Edwina drifted. The pain was still in her joints. Her youngest daughter continued to stroke her hand and it was a comfort having some human touch.

"Thank you, Nessa." Edwina was grateful to have her baby with her and used her family nickname to show her appreciation.

"So, Dr Logan was saying this morning that you would need some antibiotics for the urine infection." Vanessa decided to push on with trying to get Edwina to understand she was poorly.

"Dr Logan?" Edwina was confused. Her doctor was Dr Cameron. A lovely gentleman, proper doctor. He'd delivered Diana and was always ready to stop and have a cup of tea and a piece of cake.

"What did Dr Cameron say?"

Vanessa looked perturbed. Dr Cameron had been the family doctor before she was born and had been pushing up daisies for at least forty years.

"Dr Logan, the lady doctor you saw on Monday," she repeated in the hope that Edwina would remember the conversation from a few minutes ago.

"The urine infection is probably why you have been so poorly for the last few days."

"Urine infection? Where on earth would I have picked that up from?"

Vanessa smiled. Trust her mother to assume that you picked up an infection from somewhere. The tone of her voice suggested she was somewhat displeased with the idea that she was unhygienic in her personal cleanliness.

"I don't think it's the sort of thing you 'catch.' More importantly though, your Vitamin D is very low. It can affect your joints, cause confusion, so that's probably contributed to why you've been feeling so under the weather."

From the other side of the curtain dividing Edwina's bed from Vera Lynn, a booming voice penetrated their conversation.

"Now hang on a minute, young lady." The curtain was thrust aside, causing both mother and daughter to jump. Even the young chap across the way looked up from his phone to see what was going on.

"Just stop. There's no point you trying to frighten your mother. Vitamin D, indeed. Utter rubbish. Don't you worry, m'dear, this is all nonsense."

Vanessa stared at this corpulent man, towering over her mother's bedside, casting distain on her comments and alluding to her trying to upset Edwina.

"Excuse me? I don't believe you were a party to this conversation, or indeed the one I had with the GP this morning."

In her experience, many people viewed doctors as god-like creatures, always right in their pronouncements, who revelled in the adoration of their patients. Vanessa, however, had worked with the best in the business over the years. They neither frightened her, nor did she hold them in awe.

"Utter poppycock. Not sure what this GP was trying to do, but evidently you are only interested in frightening your mother. Let's get her home and leave her be."

With that, he turned on his heel, and exited the ward, trailing junior staff and a nurse in his wake. Vera Lynn had obviously been forgotten and looked a little perplexed that she had been deserted.

Vanessa bit back the tears. She was fully prepared to be wrong but his casual dismissal of them and their concern for their mother, coupled with the accusations of trying to frighten Edwina had hit home.

"I'll see where Diana has got to with that tea," and she scuttled from the ward.

As soon as she was out of sight of her mother, she started shaking. Diana came round the corner with one weak looking cup of tea—a greyish tinge that frankly didn't look like it had seen any sign of tea leaves or bag.

She went to say something to her sister about the tea facilities and stopped. She could tell Vanessa was upset.

"Nessa, what's up, what's happened?"

Vanessa covered her eyes with her hands, pinching the bridge of her nose and trying to stop the tears flowing.

Diana put the tea down on the floor and enveloped her sister in a hug.

"Is it that arse of a consultant?"

Vanessa nodded, then let out a frustrated growl.

"He's a twat. Didn't even bother to introduce himself and accuses us of trying to frighten her. Just told me that everything the GP had said this morning is rubbish and there's nothing wrong with Mummy. She now thinks she can just go home and go back to normal. He doesn't even seem to recognise that she can't lift herself out of a chair. How's she going to cope on her own? She winces every time she moves."

Vanessa took a deep breath and closed her eyes for a minute. Wiping her face, she looked at her sister.

"So, what do we do now?"

"Let's give her this cup of shite and find someone to talk to about what happens next." On re-entering the ward, Edwina had pulled herself up in bed and was looking around. "Here's your tea, Mummy," Diana placed the polystyrene cup on the tray table.

"Thank you." Edwina had slipped back into formal mode and was looking as bad tempered as earlier.

"Well, when am I leaving?"

"We need to speak with the nurses and find out, but I'm not sure if it will be today or tomorrow."

Diana took the lead in the discussion as Vanessa was quietly picking at her nails in the corner. She was still smarting from 'Arseface' and his assassination of her character. "And why can't I go now?" Edwina demanded.

"I need to get your father's dinner on."

Oh God, Diana thought, *she's going loopy.* Thinking on her feet, Diana explained that the paperwork needed to be done and signed and they had to wait until all that was sorted. "We'll sort out dinner," she said and picking up their coats and bags, nodded towards her sister.

"We'll see you in a bit," and bending down kissed her mother's cheek. "Get some rest and we'll be back in a bit."

They exited the ward, found a nurse who said nothing had been done about releasing Edwina and she'd be kept for another night.

Come back tomorrow was the instruction.

Both walked out of the hospital main entrance, across the car park. They paid the parking ticket and on exiting the barrier, looked at each other.

"Right," Diana said, "the pub I think for a white wine and plan of action."

Chapter 7

Saturday morning dawned with a watery reddish tinge to the December sky. Vanessa sat alone in her conservatory nursing a cup of tea. She stared out of the window. Some bluetits were enjoying breakfast courtesy of one of her many bird feeders hanging in the hedge that divided their garden from the neighbours. They lived in a quiet road with a dead end and neighbours who generally kept themselves to themselves. It suited Vanessa—she couldn't abide the idea of people just dropping in unannounced and knowing your business. As she gazed out of the window, she was grateful for the peace and quiet. Her head was still whirling with thoughts, questions and emotions but just for a few minutes, she could marvel at the acrobatics of the birds attempting to snaffle a peanut before being dive bombed by another winged companion.

The door flew open and Dan was dragged through by an over-excited Simba.

"Stop pulling! Bloody dog."

As usual, the Labrador looked at him with what could only be described as a grin round his chops. His back-end was wiggling at a rhythmic beat that would have delighted most professionals in any Strictly Come Dancing performance. He launched himself at Vanessa. He'd missed her the last few days and was out of sorts because his routine was in flux. Vanessa couldn't help but laugh. His exuberant licking and prancing was a reminder that a bit of healthy loonery would, just for a few minutes, be a balm to her agitated thoughts. "Do you want a cuppa?"

"Yeah, thanks, it's pretty chilly out there this morning."

She moved into the kitchen whilst Dan removed his boots and coat. Simba followed her looking like an obedient gun dog at the heel of his mistress but they both knew he thought milk was in the offing and if so, he'd be expecting a sample in his bowl.

She waited for the kettle to boil, absent-mindedly putting a teabag in a large mug and pouring some semi skimmed into Simba's bowl. He darted between her legs and started lapping away. Vanessa sighed, if only everything was as simple as in a dog's life—eat, sleep, walk and poo.

"You ok?" Dan came up behind her and wrapped his arms round her. He dropped a kiss on her head and she leaned back into his chest.

"Not really, it's all a bit shitty."

She stirred the milk into his tea and handed him the mug.

"What time are you going in?"

"About two. I said I'd collect Diana on the way through. She messaged earlier. The ward said Mummy had a reasonable night but nothing about her being discharged. We'll see what they say this afternoon."

After a quick sandwich, she drove away from the house, Dan waving her goodbye on the doorstep. She stopped at the newsagents, picking up a couple of magazines for her mother. There wasn't any point getting her flowers, she'd sort something out when they'd got her home. A quick pit stop at

44

Diana's to use the toilet and the two women set off for the hospital.

They managed to find a parking space and joined the ramshackle groups of people heading in via the main entrance. Some clasped baskets of fruit or flowers, others had balloons announcing 'It's a Boy!' and some evidently were doing duty visits and just put their heads down and barrelled through the sea of visitors.

Diana had learned that Edwina was in Oak Ward when she'd called in the morning, and they made their way along the echo-y corridors. There was an overpowering aroma of hospital disinfectant and boiled veg. They didn't speak but followed the signs, weaving left and right along endless internal roadways.

They saw Edwina before she saw them. Sitting alongside her bed in a ward of six others, she was swamped by her pink and purple dralon dressing gown. Her hair was tangled and gave her a wild appearance. She was agitatedly wringing her fingers, fiddling with her wedding ring whilst her eyes darted to and fro.

"Hello." Diana leaned across the lap table her mother was sitting behind. She placed a kiss on her mother's head and moved aside, so Vanessa could reach her. They were both braced for another matriarchal onslaught of indignation at still being unable to get home. Edwina grabbed her daughters' hands.

"Oh, girls, you're safe."

"Er yes, we're fine. How are you feeling today?"

Edwina ignored her middle daughter.

"I've been so worried. I didn't know where you were. They sent a ransom note after you disappeared last night but we couldn't find you."

They looked at one another. Diana's eyes said 'bloody hell, she's gone ga-ga.' She motioned her sister to sit in the only available chair. She needed to gather her thoughts for a minute as this had thrown her.

"I'll go and find another chair," and she disappeared down the corridor. Edwina held Vanessa's hand tightly and she gently stroked her mother's hand. "Where did they take you?"

Fortunately, for Vanessa there was no need to answer as her mother was in full flow.

"I didn't pay any money but they took all my jam. I've hidden some in the safe though, so if they come back, we'll have to move it. It's strawberry. You can't get strawberry any more. You won't give it away will you?"

Vanessa was torn between wanting to howl with laughter or burst into tears. It was clear Edwina was having some sort of breakdown but the desperation with which she was clinging to her hand, gave her cause to think she must reassure her mother.

"Well, it's all sorted now and you can see we're both fine. Everyone sends their love. Dan's been walking Simba this morning. Said it was pretty chilly outside. The children are all fine and I think they're Christmas shopping this weekend."

She was conscious she was rambling as much as her mother but hoped that having a reasonably sensible conversation about family would bring her mother back to normality. Diana reappeared with a chair and looked enquiringly at her sister. Vanessa gave a slight shake of her head and a wide-eyed 'not sure what's happening here' look.

"I was just saying, it's chilly and lots of people are out Christmas shopping."

Diana took the hint and continued.

"Yes, pretty blustery out there." She motioned to the window where the trees were bending and dancing in the wind.

"Where are we?" Edwina looked puzzled. There was an aroma of ammonia arising from the vicinity of their mother's chair and there was no evidence of a catheter in place. "Eastbourne. You're in Eastbourne Hospital, remember you came in a couple of days ago."

"No, it's not Eastbourne." Edwina exclaimed. "They're not Eastbourne trees."

Both Vanessa and Diana looked at one another and were, for a minute, lost for anything to say.

Vanessa then decided on the only option that immediately came to mind. "Would you like a cup of tea, Mummy?" Tea, that sorted everything, right!

"That'd be lovely, darling, thank you."

"Tea or coffee?" She asked her sister.

"Coffee, thanks." Diana replied.

"Ok, I'll pop to the coffee shop, won't be long."

Vanessa shot out of the ward door. Her mother's incoherent ramblings had shaken her. She was turning senile overnight.

She returned from the café with one hot cup of tea and two cinnamon lattes, one with soya milk. The specialist coffee was a nod to the approaching celebration of Christmas and allowed them to charge more for the privilege but there was something comforting in the milky drink that smelt of all the best bits of the Yuletide. She'd also purchased a slice of lemon drizzle cake and a chocolate muffin.

"Thought we could share these and have ourselves a little tea party."

Edwina giggled. In Vanessa's absence, Diana had combed her mother's hair in a vain attempt to make her less ghost-like. Edwina sipped her tea. Both noticed her hands shaking.

"So, how are the children? Are Mark and Ruth coming for Christmas?"

This sudden change of behaviour and style of conversation threw her daughters. Diana cautiously answered.

"Mark's coming over on his own. Ruth hasn't got any holiday left, so unfortunately, she won't be here until next year."

Diana's son lived in America with his wife. They lived in New York and he was a political journalist. Ruth worked for a realtor but their holiday entitlement was pretty rubbish, so trips to the UK were infrequent, though Michael and Diana tried to visit them at least once a year.

Edwina clearly remembered he wasn't in this country and she seemed to have flipped back to her normal self.

"That's a shame, he loves Christmas. All the excitement of the presents and turkey, not to mention the board games and mince pies."

Diana visibly relaxed. Her mother had just summed up her only child accurately and with great recollection of his joy at the seasonal festivities.

"How's he getting here?" Edwina was tucking into a morsel of lemon drizzle cake and the crumbs clung to the sides of her mouth. Without her dentures, the folds of skin around her lower face were emphasised.

"He'll get a flight from New York on the 23rd, so should be over his jetlag by Christmas Day."

"A flight?" Edwina looked puzzled. "Why does he need a flight? Surely, Father Christmas will just be able to drop him off on his way through?"

Okaaay, thought Diana, *and we're back in La La Land.* She knew she was gaping at her mother but somehow couldn't think of a suitable retort. She would have laughed, but Edwina had said this with such conviction but in such a normal conversational voice that it completely stumped Diana how she should respond.

Vanessa came to the rescue.

"So, I see they've put up some Christmas decorations here. It's lovely they make the effort for everyone."

Her mother looked distracted and then beamed a smile.

"They all work so hard for Christmas, and the ship's decked out with tinsel and baubles. Daddy is going to carve the turkey for all the men and he's given them a tot of rum for the afternoon." She had dropped her voice to a conspiratorial whisper, evidently not wanting her daughters to spill the beans.

It proved too much for Vanessa.

"Well, you're looking a bit tired. Do you want to have a lie down?"

"In a bit, dear, I'll sit here a while. Thank you for coming. I'll see you at home after Christmas. Daddy and I are going away whilst he's on leave, so I won't be around till the New Year."

Gently, they kissed their mother's cheek and squeezed her hand. "We'll see you soon, get some rest."

"Goodbye, dears, thank you again."

With that, Edwina sat back and nibbled the remains of the chocolate muffin.

Diana returned the chair to the corridor. A tired looking nurse was inputting something into her computer at the nurses' station.

"Excuse me, could you give us an update on Edwina?" Diana was pleasant but authoritative. "Who?" She said absently.

"Edwina Thompson, Bay 6, our mother."

The effects of the afternoon's interaction were beginning to tell on both women. The nurse looked up for a fleeting second, debated a sarcastic reply but something about the faces of the two middle aged women in front of her, caused her to stop typing and fully focus on them.

"We're treating her urine infection with antibiotics. Her shoulder seems painful but it's unrelated to any infection."

"She's very confused. Has she been like it all day?"

The nurse answered in a roundabout fashion.

"UTIs often cause the elderly to be confused. Once the medication is working, she'll be right as rain."

"Has she had a shower?" Diana was conscious that her mother was not as fragrant as she'd like to be. Usually, Edwina was awash with her favourite 'Coty' talc and perfume but the aroma of stale urine seemed to be all she was bathed in at present.

"Not sure. She pulled her catheter out yesterday evening, so she can definitely have one if she wants."

It wasn't the reassurance they were looking for.

"She probably needs some help getting to the shower. She's not steady on her feet without her stick."

"Feel free to use the shower when you visit her," and with that the young woman returned to her keyboard.

Diana bristled, but Vanessa laid a hand on her arm. Not one for confrontation, or indeed with a wish to have their mother marked as a woman with a trouble-making family, she cautioned Diana.

"Let's leave it for now. See how she is tomorrow. We can always help her then or she might be home by then and we can sort it out there."

She said it loud enough for the nurse to be aware of the conversation but she gave no indication of having heard.

They looked back, waved at Edwina who was busy picking at an imaginary thread on her dressing gown and both wearily headed for the hospital exit.

Chapter 8

Sunday dawned with that perfect December combination of hard frost, chill air but brilliant sunshine and cloudless skies. Vanessa and Dan had breakfasted in bed. It sounded luxurious but in reality, was a couple of bits of toast and marmalade, a hot cup of tea and Simba stretched across their legs. He had his eyes closed in the pretence of sleep, but was alert to the opportunity of a dropped piece of toast.

The bedroom TV was tuned into the breakfast show but Vanessa wasn't paying much attention. On top of all the events of the last few days at the hospital, she was conscious she'd not been in the office much, though Dan had been keeping on top of things. Caitlin and Sam were waiting to exchange contracts on their new house but she couldn't see that happening before Christmas. Solicitors wouldn't be in a hurry to work extensively over the festive season. She knew she was fretting about something over which she had no control but it gave her a focus to vent some frustration that was really directed at the helplessness she felt about Edwina. She had the sense of being on a runaway train and it was beyond her ability to take back control.

Aware that Dan was staring at her she turned, realising he'd obviously said something that required a response from her.

"Mmm, sorry?"

"I said, how about we give Simba a good walk this morning and then head to Diana's? Caitlin can pop in and feed him tonight if we're back late and she can whizz him round the block."

"Ok, sounds like a plan. I'll get a shower." With a weary resignation, she swung her legs out of the bed, patted Simba and headed to the family bathroom. Whilst they had an en-suite shower room, now it was just the two of them, it made sense to use the bathroom as her own private enclave. There was the opportunity to put out some scented candles, a bath cushion when she wanted a soak and other 'namby pamby' stuff as Dan phrased it. A pet hate of his was the throw cushions she insisted on putting on their bed each morning. They'd had numerous conversations about how useless they were versus the aesthetic look they presented. He was a practical chap who didn't like unnecessary fuss. All he needed was shampoo, shower gel and toothbrush to furnish his morning ablutions. As he eloquently put it. "I'm off for a shit, shower and shave." He'd first used the phrase early in their relationship and it had stuck—so much so that even the kids would chime, "Dad's off for his 3 S's."

An hour later, they'd had a decent walk around the local fields. A dose of fresh air and Vanessa was feeling a bit more with it. Simba had sniffed his way round the park and surrounding wheatfields. They were currently bare, with forlorn sticks sticking out of the ground as a reminder of their blanket of summer abundance, with gold waving fronds before the harvest. At the moment, the ground was boggy and soggy. *Winter could be so depressing,* Vanessa thought. Everything dying and covered in mud. If she'd been in a more positive mood, she'd have said everything was sleeping till Spring. But she wanted the chance to wallow in self-pity for a bit and there was the dawning realisation that Edwina was drawing to the end of her life. It was something you anticipated of course with older parents. What was disturbing to Vanessa though was that whilst they'd all expected it, probably since their father's death over twenty years ago, it seemed now to be a very real possibility in the coming weeks or months. The downright weirdness of the previous day's conversation with their mother had frightened her and was constantly playing on her mind. She wasn't sure she was ready to be an orphan. She might be fifty-one and feeling middle aged at times but your parents were a constant in that time and she recognised that very soon there would be a seismic shift in the status quo.

Later that afternoon, both sisters and their spouses arrived on the ward. Edwina was still in her dressing gown, sitting where she had been the day before alongside her bed. Today, she had the *Sunday Express* open on her table. She prided herself on doing the daily crossword to keep her mind active.

She smiled at the foursome who exchanged kisses with her and the two men went off in search of more chairs. It was obvious she was improving. She knew them all. There were no odd conversations about trees or Father Christmas and she remembered the doctor had been round that morning.

"They say I can go home tomorrow." She was obviously delighted.

Mindful that when they'd had this conversation a couple of days ago, neither of her daughters had been enthusiastic, they made sure this time they sounded positive and upbeat.

"That's great news."

"Be nice to be back in your own bed."

Dan and Michael sat and talked to her whilst the sisters found a nurse at the station. It wasn't their chirpy friend from yesterday, so that was a positive. She confirmed that Edwina would be released the following day, probably late morning or early afternoon.

No care package was needed but she'd have some antibiotics to clear up the urine infection.

On their way back to the car park after visiting time ended, the four agreed a plan of action for the next day. Michael was working, so Diana would collect Edwina whilst Dan and Vanessa would go straight to her house, open up, put the heating on and get some food in, so she wouldn't need to worry about anything for a few days. They agreed they'd take it in turns to stay with her though neither could do the first night. It was certain Edwina would be exhausted and probably just sleep until they could get there early the following morning. They'd ask Edith to pop in and check her first thing and Diana could be there for 8:30.

Having sorted the arrangements, they parted company and returned to their own homes for the evening.

Later that night, Vanessa sat in front of the TV with a glass of wine in her hand and the remnants of a Chinese takeaway on her lap. She wasn't paying much attention to the programme but the opportunity to relax for a while and know things were returning to normal was a huge weight off her shoulders.

Chapter 9

The car pulled up on the driveway and Edwina sighed gratefully. Back home at last.

The doorway opened and Vanessa and Dan both walked down the pathway. Diana got out and looking somewhat frazzled went round to the passenger door. Dan bent down to his mother in law's level.

"Welcome home, let's get you out and settled with a cuppa."

"She's quite stiff," Diana warned him as he leant into the doorway and took Edwina's arm.

She gave a shout of pain. He leapt back, somewhat alarmed.

"It's my shoulder, I've slept badly on it," she explained.

Diana rolled her eyes. They all knew it was nothing to do with sleeping on it. She'd had a painful shoulder for months, long before Caitlin and Sam's wedding in September, yet she persisted in this ridiculous show of pretence.

"Hellooo." Beryl and Stan, her immediate neighbours in the close were on their way out and crossed their immaculate lawn, heading in the direction of Diana's car.

Edwina almost visibly shrank in her seat as if she was trying to be invisible.

Diana cut off their approach with a business-like focus that brooked no further interaction.

"Hi, just arrived back from hospital, so we're getting her settled. Bye."

God, these people are nosey, she thought. Turning her attention back to her mother, she saw Dan had somehow managed to swing her legs out of the little Ka car. Supporting her 'good' side, she half levered, half dragged herself out. Stick in hand, she started up the path but it was clear she'd never get up the large entrance step at the front door.

"I'll open up the back door." Vanessa scooted past her mother and raced through the hallway to the back entrance, unlocking the door and pinning it back. She completed her action in the time it took Edwina to shuffle the 10 paces from front door to back gate.

Eventually inside the house, she again sighed with relief and was in her favourite armchair with a cup of tea and a biscuit. The electric fire was on and Vanessa and Dan had arrived early, putting the heating on and getting the bed aired with an electric blanket so it was at least warm from the December chill that was in the air.

Edwina closed her eyes and the three of them went into the kitchen.

"Her antibiotics weren't available," said Diana. "I spent just over an hour at the hospital pharmacy but they didn't have enough for her! The ward sister gave me enough for today and tonight from the drugs trolley and said if I go back in the morning, they'll be ready. She was very apologetic, but it was a complete cock-up. At least she has some to see her through tonight."

She took a sip of her tea and looked disconsolate.

"I'm not sure how she's going to cope on her own."

They'd both tried to persuade Edwina to stay with one of them for a few days but she'd resisted, saying she couldn't manage the stairs in their homes. Despite the offer of making a bed downstairs, and they both had downstairs toilets, they recognised the stubborn streak that Edwina employed when she'd made up her mind. That said, they could both relate to the desire to be in your own bed, surrounded by your own things, so they did understand. It would really have just been easier on them.

"I've got some Complan in and thought we could make up a flask of tea. She can have that by the bed and if she has some soup and toast before we leave, we can get her into bed. She should then hopefully be ok till the morning. I've asked Edith to come in first thing to give her a cup of tea and I can be here by nine. If you get the drugs from the hospital, we can spend tomorrow with her and work out a timetable for cover for the next few days till she starts improving." Vanessa paused for breath. They all sipped their tea in silence.

Edwina sat in her favourite armchair by the fireplace, eyes closed, head back with a view of her garden. The quiet ticking of the clock was a familiar sound and the murmur of her daughters' voices in the kitchen floated through the open doorway though she couldn't make out what they were saying.

Oh, the relief to be home. Edwina, as an only child, and the wife of a merchant seaman who had so often been away for months at a time, was content with her own company. Of course, she had friends—less now that they were all shuffling off this mortal coil, or they'd gone doolally with age. Approaching her ninety-third year, she never saw herself as an old lady but wasn't averse to playing the poor widow woman when it suited her.

Friends; they were more of acquaintances now. Neighbours, people she'd know around the town for over fifty years or more. Not close confidantes, but thinking about it now, maybe she'd never really had those sort of relationships. Family was everything to her.

That and maintaining respectability. Jennifer's antics over the years had forced Edwina, and to some extent James, to be cautious about sharing family tribulations with outsiders, no matter how friendly they appeared.

Edwina wasn't stupid. She knew she was ill. She wasn't sure exactly what the problem was, but at her age, she knew it wasn't trivial. If everyone would just leave her alone, she could slip away, quietly and with no fuss. There certainly wasn't going to be a repeat of that hospital admission. Incessant shouting, constant talking, people poking at her, measuring this and that, speaking to her like she was some sort of imbecilic retarded child! Diana would be shocked if she heard her mother use those terms. She didn't appreciate that Edwina was from a different generation and what the girls found embarrassing and offensive, their mother thought they were just being overly sensitive.

She wished they'd go away. They were still talking in the kitchen. She coughed and they both appeared, as she knew they would. They were good girls and she loved them dearly but now she wanted them to go and leave her alone with her own thoughts.

"How do you feel?" Vanessa asked.

"Better for being home," her mother replied. "You should all get off now."

"I'll stay for a while, help you into bed, you look exhausted." Diana took the tea cup from her mother's hand.

Edwina couldn't deny it and maybe if she got into bed they'd all bugger off.

Vanessa and Dan packed everything up and left, promising to return the following morning.

Diana helped her mother into the bedroom. Her twin bed looked so inviting. Getting her mother undressed and into some fresh nightclothes took longer than she thought and whilst she would have liked to give her mother a bath or shower, there was no way she'd be able to climb into the bath today, so they'd have to leave that for maybe when both sisters were there.

The bathroom across the hallway from Edwina's bedroom looked a very long way away. It took all her strength to walk from one to the other. Diana went to come in with her. "I'm fine, thank you." Edwina looked hard at her daughter, daring her to argue.

Fortunately, she took the message, retreating to the bedroom, setting up a flask of Complan and another of tea. She popped some toast in the toaster in the kitchen and returning to the bedroom, removed the heated blanket and slipped a hot water bottle towards the foot of the bed. She found the hands-free telephone in the study and placed it on her mother's bedside table. They tried to get her to use a mobile phone a couple of years ago but she'd resolutely refused to entertain the idea, deliberately allowing it to run out of battery. It sat uncharged and lifeless on the mantelpiece, a reminder to them that if Edwina chose not to co-operate, no amount of coercion would make her change her mind.

In the bathroom, Edwina lowered herself gingerly onto the toilet. Everything ached and hurt. Even her skin seemed fragile and she bit her lip to keep from crying out.

She 'spent a penny.' Such a strange saying but it sat well with her Edwardian upbringing and kept things tasteful.

The bright red blood in the pan was anything but tasteful.

She wasn't sure what it meant but it wasn't the first time it had happened and even she knew there was a working assumption that any blood couldn't be good. She was grateful Diana had left the room.

She tidied herself up, flushed the toilet, making sure there were no tell-tale traces of red left and straightened herself.

Catching sight of herself in the bathroom mirror, she looked sad. Her once beautiful thick auburn hair was now completely white. It had lacked attention in the last few days with no sign of a brush or comb having passed through it. The wispy strands gave her a somewhat wild, banshee appearance. Her deep brown eyes were sunken into her pale face, skin that was papery thin and wrinkled.

Good God, she thought, *I look like a walking corpse.* Pulling a comb from the bathroom drawer, she made the best she could of tidying her hair, though the aches and pains in her shoulders and arms prevented her from raising them to tackle the birds nest atop her head.

"Sod it," she thought, *it'll have to wait.*

Setting off back to the bedroom, Diana grasped her arm and helped guide her to the bed. Gingerly, she sat down again, slipping off her red slippers and took the two tablets her daughter was holding out for her with some water. Her antibiotics, which she dutifully swallowed. She then managed to swing her legs up as she pivoted round. It was a similar move to the one she'd done to get out of the car, but in reverse and the effort caused her to flop back onto the bed.

Bliss, sheer bliss, to be back in her own bed.

The afternoon sun was setting, so Diana pulled the lavender velvet curtains shut. The radiator alongside her bed was warm and the girls' thoughtfulness of the heated blanket and water bottle meant she was wrapped in a cosy cocoon. It was an oasis of comfort after the trauma of the last few days.

"There's tea and a flask of Complan here. That should keep you going if you need something in the night. I've done a slice of toast and there's a plate of biscuits too."

After her sister had left, Diana had tried to persuade her mother to have some soup and sandwiches but she said she'd had a big lunch at the hospital and wasn't hungry. Actually, she couldn't remember if she had but she really didn't want anything and it kept the girls from fussing.

She just wanted to sleep now.

"Nessa will be here first thing and I'll come over as soon as I've got your antibiotics from the hospital. If you need anything, the phone's there and we've asked Edith to pop in early to give you a cup of tea. I won't ring tonight in case you are asleep. Do you want the radio on?"

Her mother shook her head slightly.

"Thank you, darling, you've been an angel, I'll just get some rest."

Diana looked down at the small, frail figure in the bed. Her gutsy, belligerent, and at times, frustrating, mother was there somewhere but Diana caught her breath, realising that probably for the first time, Edwina's time was drawing to a close. Maybe not today or this week, but before too long, the natural order would be followed and she would slip away.

Edwina could drive Diana mad. In truth, they were very similar with a liking to be in control and right. This often led to them clashing but they were very dear to each other and she didn't like to see her mother laid so low.

Diana bent down, kissing her mother's forehead, as Edwina squeezed her hand. "Sleep well, we'll see you tomorrow."

She slipped out of the back door, locking Edwina in and walked to her car on the driveway. Some tough decisions were going to have to be made in the coming days.

Inside the bungalow, Edwina revelled in the peace. The light from next door's kitchen could faintly be seen through the curtains but she was home, warm and in her own bed. *Let's hope I don't see tomorrow,* she thought to herself and drifted into an unconscious sleep.

Chapter 10

Vanessa and Diana both supported Edwina's arms as they eased her off the commode. The bright red contents of the pan registered on both their faces at the same time and they looked at each other in alarm.

The nurse, standing alongside them, looked as shocked as they did. Edwina just looked exhausted.

"How long has she been passing blood like this?"

"We've no idea." Vanessa spoke low but urgently as they moved Edwina gently back onto the A&E couch.

"All I can tell you is she wasn't passing blood when her catheter was in last week."

"When last week? What catheter?" The petite nurse was writing on the chart. She looked up at Vanessa's reply.

"She was admitted last Thursday after she'd collapsed at home. You catheterised her here in A&E and she was sent home yesterday. The ambulance was called again this morning when her neighbour found her on the floor."

"You mean she was discharged in this state?"

"Basically, yes." Diana was settling Edwina as best she could. Once again, their mother was in a cubicle, shivering in her dressing gown and whilst not confused as she had been at the weekend, she was obviously weak and struggling with the events of the last few hours.

"I'm calling the urology team. I'll be back." And with that, the nurse disappeared. Edwina's daughters covered her with their coats in a bid to warm her up.

She was fretful, wanting repeatedly to use the commode and then falling into a restless doze.

Earlier that morning, Vanessa had received a frantic call from Edith to say Edwina was again on her way to hospital via ambulance. She found her half in and half out of bed, disorientated and slurring her speech.

Diana, who had been in the hospital pharmacy, waiting for her mother's antibiotics to be dispensed, had gone straight to A&E when she got the call and met Vanessa an hour later when her sister arrived at the hospital.

X-rays had followed with Edwina rallying for a while and complaining she needed to get home, but the effort of having several x-rays and spending a couple of hours on a trolley in the corridor had weakened her resolve.

Whilst both Vanessa and Diana had been annoyed at her apparent insistence at going home, they recognised this as fear on their mother's part and their anger was misdirected, really being aimed at the situation they found themselves in once again.

She'd been moved to a cubicle a couple of hours previously and since then, had intermittently had nurses coming in, promising to be with her shortly...but they were very busy.

The two women sat in the small cubicle. Taking turns to use the one solitary plastic chair whilst the other stood or sat on the floor, they kept up a chatter of inane conversation to pass the time, routinely stroking Edwina's hand and giving her sips of water.

After another hour or so, just as Diana was on the verge of yet again trying to find someone, a young doctor pushed aside the curtains.

Introducing himself as Dr Curry from the urological team, he started taking a history from Edwina. It soon became clear to everyone, excluding her, that she was lapsing into previous nonsensical conversations. She talked about her husband coming home from sea later that day as Vanessa stood behind her, shaking her head at the doctor and indicating that their father was no longer alive. Edwina claimed the blood she had passed was really just a heavy period.

Dr Curry patted her hand, told her to rest and with an inclination of his head, got Vanessa and Diana to follow him outside.

Taking a more concise and factual medical history from Vanessa, he concluded that there was something more serious going on than just a urine infection.

"Passing blood in that quantity is always alarming, so we need to rule out what may be the cause. Not knowing how long this has been happening isn't helpful, but we'll get some scans and bloods done and review her. She'll be in a few days."

With that, he waved a cheery goodbye to Edwina and disappeared up the corridor.

"So what happens now?" Diana asked the nurse.

"We'll need to get her onto a medical ward but that may take a few hours. I'm going to see if we can at least get her settled in the day unit for now, so she's in a proper bed and then we'll transfer her as soon as possible. There's not much more you can do. Go home, get some rest and ring in later. Ask for A&E Reception and we can let you know which ward she has gone to."

Thanking her for everything, the three of them entered the cubicle.

"Righto, Edwina, my love, I'm going to find you a comfy bed and a cuppa so you can rest up. I'm sending the girls away for some dinner and we'll keep them posted."

Vanessa smiled—this tiny little nurse who was definitely young enough to be Edwina's granddaughter had taken charge and you weren't going to argue with her.

They collected their bits and pieces, making sure Edwina had her handbag and reading glasses to hand. Not that she needed either, but they knew it would comfort her.

"My keys, where are my keys?"

"They're in your bag, Mummy." Diana jangled the back door key from the depths of her bag and Edwina visibly relaxed closing her eyes.

"We'll see you later," they said, taking it in turns to kiss her forehead.

"Goodbye, girls, thank you so much, you're such good girls."

And with that, they swallowed hard and left the cubicle.

Diana stopped by the nurses' desk as the young girl was trying to locate a bed in the day unit.

"I'm not sure if you need to know, but Mummy has a Living Will."

It felt morbid and somewhat disloyal bringing this up but Diana knew it was best to do this now.

"Oh definitely, we'll need a copy for her records."

Ever efficient, Diana took her copy out of her bag.

"Here's my copy if you want to photocopy it before we go."

"Unfortunately, we need the original. Bureaucracy, I know, but if you can bring that in, that would be great."

"She's got that in her bag," Vanessa said, realising this was going to be a difficult manoeuvre without explaining in detail to Edwina what they needed.

"Hang on," and she slipped back into the cubicle where Edwina lay with her eyes closed. Reaching for her bag, Vanessa opened the clasp and there in the side pocket, was the document in its see-through bag. Strictly speaking, it was an old plastic wrapping from a pair of stockings, but Edwina was renowned for not throwing away anything that could be reused—she would never recognise herself as a 'green warrior' but a lifetime of 'making do and mending' meant that she repurposed all sorts of things that many would throw away. This included plastic wrappings for her American Tan stockings!

Edwina stirred, opened her eyes and looked directly at Vanessa with her deep brown eyes. The look said 'just what do you think you are doing?'

"Sorry, Mummy." She patted her hand and smoothly said, "Run out of change for the car park. I'm borrowing a pound coin, if that's ok?"

Uncomfortable with the ease of the lie, she took a coin from her mother's purse whilst slipping the small plastic document into her pocket.

Edwina was generous to a fault, always wanting to pay her way, especially for things like petrol or parking if her girls took her out, so she naturally demurred, relaxing and closing her eyes again.

Vanessa slipped back out, gave the original Living Will to the nurse who immediately copied it, returning the letter to Vanessa and clipping the photocopy into Edwina's A&E records.

"How are you going to put it back?" Her sister enquired with a raised eyebrow. "I'll do it tomorrow when she's distracted. At least we know they've got it."

Thanking the various A&E staff they'd been talking to virtually all day, both women went to the car park pay machine at the hospital exit.

By chance, they'd parked close to each other. They exited the building into the dark winter afternoon, leaving behind the newly decorated Xmas tree in the hospital reception area.

"Do you want to stay at ours tonight?" Diana asked as she rummaged in her bag for her keys, holding her parking exit ticket between her teeth.

When Vanessa didn't answer, she looked up and saw tears pouring down the face of her younger sibling.

Dropping her bag to the ground, she wrapped her arms around Vanessa, who returned the hug and the two of them stood, silently crying together. Long hours in cold cubicles, constant waiting and a sense of helplessness culminated in them both releasing the emotions of the day on each other's shoulders.

"This is shitty," Vanessa stated, wiping her eyes and nose with the back of her hand. "I know, but we'll get through it together. Back to ours?"

Wearily, Vanessa nodded, grateful not to have to make the long drive home. They'd kept their husbands updated throughout the day and Dan had already suggested that his wife stay with her sister overnight.

"Takeaway?" Vanessa volunteered. "My treat."

"Blimey, they'll be making good money out of us this last week," Diana said. "You ok to drive?"

Nodding, Vanessa said she'd follow her sister back. Getting into her car, she took a deep breath. The lights from the hospital windows lit up the dark skies. She didn't like the thought of leaving Edwina there and who knew if she'd make it through the night, but they had no choice.

Inserting the key into the ignition, she turned the engine on her car, easing out of the space and followed Diana towards the exit barrier. Deciding to ring Dan when she'd eaten, she tuned into the radio, listening to the news bulletin which provided her company on the journey.

Chapter 11

"You need to come and calm her down."

Diana had taken the call from the hospital just as she and Vanessa had settled to watch some TV.

Edwina had been in hospital now for five days. She'd been moved onto a medical ward and had endured a round of 'poking and prodding' from various medics. She remained in a state of confusion—some days, she was just tired and resigned, accepting they were endeavouring to find an answer to her ongoing debility, but on other days, she was argumentative, determine to get home and frequently referencing her long dead mother and husband who needed their dinner!

Every day, Vanessa and Diana went in to sit with her. Unsure of the temperament they'd find her in, it was emotionally draining for them both. Michael was working away for a few days and Dan was holding the fort in the office. Running his own building firm, with Vanessa working as the office manager, he spent his days doing quotes and site visits now more than getting his hands dirty. December was a quiet time of the year for the business, so it wasn't difficult for him to cope alone and Simba was getting his fair share of long walks.

It allowed the sisters to concentrate all their energies on Edwina. This afternoon, they'd taken in a new dressing gown for her. Shorter than her old purple padded job, and lovely and fleecy, they felt there was less chance of her falling over the hem. She'd been grateful of course, but was so very tired. Conscious the girls were chatting amiably, she had dozed intermittently, eyes closed, biting down on the inside of her bottom lip as the irritation and the burning pain from her bladder gnawed away at her groin, back and sides. She'd eventually persuaded them to leave and had sunk back onto the flimsy hospital pillows, praying for some peace and quiet.

The two women had returned to Diana's, walked the dogs round the block in the fading winter light, marvelling at the ostentatious Christmas lights in some of the houses. It was an old family tradition to walk round the streets to work out the best light displays—there was a mix of the truly spectacular and the truly awful, but it was good to do something that felt 'normal.'

They'd returned home, settling for a sandwich and a shared bottle of white wine. Having decided on an early night, they'd gone upstairs and Vanessa had been in bed going through her work emails and Facebook page. She could hear Diana moving around in her bedroom, taking a shower in the en-suite and talking to her dogs.

The landline had rung.

It wasn't late, about 9:30 and Diana had answered without any great trepidation.

The night nurse from Edwina's ward explained she was almost hysterical. Diana could hear her mother in the background, voice raised and unusually for Edwina, in full abusive ranting flow.

"Don't you bloody touch me. Get away. Who do you think you are? I'll call the police. You dreadful man, move away or I'll hit you with my fucking stick and don't think I won't." The nurse explained they couldn't calm her. She was pacing the ward, upsetting the other patients and Vanessa and Diana would have to come and speak to her.

Diana rubbed her eyes, "Ok, we'll be there shortly. Tell her we're coming."

She clicked the off button on the phone and looked at her sister who had crossed the landing and had caught the last part of the conversation.

Diana sat on the bed, head in her hands.

"Oh God, she's going mad. I could hear her shouting in the background." Her face crumpled as she sobbed "It's not her, where's she gone?"

Vanessa sat alongside her sister, took her hands and looked into her brown eyes—a reflection of their mother's chocolate pools. "It's ok, we'll go and see her and calm her down."

"How? She's out of control, they say she expects us to take her home. How can we? We've had a drink, we can't drive."

In true Diana style, all the obstacles and worries came flooding out in one breath. "Well, I only had a glass and a bit, so I'm ok to drive." Vanessa silently thanked whoever that her dislike of Pinot Grigo meant she hadn't had much to drink and she'd actually left a fair amount, pouring it down the sink when Diana had popped to the loo. It was ridiculous really that at over fifty, she couldn't say, actually I think it's pretty shite, can I have a G&T? Now, however, she was relieved she hadn't broken open the Bombay Sapphire, otherwise it would have been a taxi to the hospital.

"But she wants us to take her home," Diana wailed.

"Well, we'll just say the doctors won't let us take her tonight. By tomorrow hopefully, she'll either have forgotten or we'll have some answers."

They arrived at the entrance to the hospital half an hour later. Edwina couldn't be seen or heard as they walked onto the ward. They managed to attract the attention of the senior nurse without having to venture too far into the main area. She came and spoke to them quietly at the swing doors that led onto the medical ward.

"She's calmer, still pacing, but much better when we said you were coming." Vanessa took charge, keeping hold of Diana's hand both for comfort and strength.

"We'll talk to her but we need to see one of her doctors first thing tomorrow. She's been here for days now and we've not had any information except they're doing tests. We need some definitive answers, so we can make plans for her."

"Ok, I'll make sure the day team know at handover. Come in tomorrow at 10 and we'll make sure someone talks to you."

The two women thanked the sister and looking at each other, they stepped forward in determined fashion to handle their errant mother.

Rounding the corner, they could see her pacing up and down by her cubicle, stick in hand, talking animatedly to herself. She saw Diana and Vanessa approach and broke into a delighted smile.

"Girls! Hello, how lovely to see you."

They were both momentarily taken aback, expecting her to be in full ranty mode at them. "Well, what's all this about?"

Diana demanded. The mix of relief that her mother was reasonable, combined with her fear of how to deal with the situation, had made her comment come out more brusque than she had intended.

"All what?" Edwina enquired. She seemed genuinely surprised to see them and for a moment, she appeared to flag and falter, as if her resolve had weakened.

Vanessa gently took her mother's arm, steering her towards the bed. Edwina didn't resist.

"The nurse called us. She was worried about you and thought you'd like to see us."

"Bless her, she's a poppet," Edwina replied as she compliantly settled on the bed.

Not the interfering two-faced bitch you were calling her an hour ago then, thought Diana. "I'd like to go home now, please." Looking up at her two daughters with pleading eyes was nearly the undoing of them both. Diana bent down, gently removing Edwina's slippers. "Of course you do." Vanessa was sat alongside her on the bed.

"It's just we're not allowed to until the doctor has said so in the morning. Once he has given us the ok, we'll have you out of here and back home."

All the while she was talking, Vanessa had eased her mother into bed, covering her with the thin sheets and blankets and her new blue fleecy dressing gown, tucked around her for extra warmth.

"Oh, that's lovely, we'll go tomorrow then," and with that Edwina lay back on her pillows and closed her eyes.

The sisters looked at each other again with incredulity— surely she wasn't giving in that easily?

Taking their cue from her relaxed demeanour, they put her handbag beside her on the coverlet, kissed her forehead and crept out, quietly drawing the curtain around her bed.

They headed for the swing door exit. The nurses weren't at their night desk, so must be dealing with another patient. However, all was now quiet, so they slipped out and down the silent hospital corridors heading back towards the entrance.

"Bloody hell," Vanessa said, "think we got away with that one."

"I need a drink," Diana retorted and for the second time that day; they headed into the car park as sleety rain started falling. It was cold and damp and both were lost in their own thoughts about what to do next.

Chapter 12

At 10 am the next morning, both Diana and Vanessa sat in the easy chairs at the entrance to the ward. Edwina had apparently had a quiet night, and seemed to be recovering from the previous evening's shenanigans by still being asleep.

Over breakfast, they'd made a list of questions for the doctor, mainly focusing on diagnosis, prognosis and discharge. This information would inform them as to the next step.

By 10:30, they were becoming anxious and not a little bit annoyed. Why did doctors always work to another timetable? They could have had to take time off work; they might have had babies to look after (or grandchildren at least), or any number of other commitments. But no, the medical profession followed the beat of its own drum and damn everyone else. Eventually, a small doctor arrived wearing faded scrubs and a pair of battered blue Crocs. "Hi, I'm Dr Saleh," and holding out his hand, shook their outstretched palms and sat down opposite them. Both noticed there was no apology for keeping them waiting!

They outlined the situation, expressly requesting information about Edwina's tests and diagnosis. Early on, Diana dropped into the conversation they held a Lasting

Power of Attorney to enable them to help with decisions around her health and personal care.

Dr Saleh nodded. "She's got persistent urine infections that aren't responding to antibiotics. We're booking an ultrasound and cystoscopy. The KUB was negative." Vanessa was concentrating on what he was saying.

With her medical background, particularly having worked for a leading urologist in her early twenties, the terminology wasn't bewildering, though she was aware that for her layman sister, he hadn't explained things at all well!

"When are you doing the cystoscopy?" She asked him, nodding to Diana to reassure her. "She's on the list for later this week. Depends really on theatre availability and any emergencies." He lowered his voice and leant in towards them.

"You need to get her out of here as soon as possible though. If she stays, she'll likely get MRSA and that'll kill her."

This revelation floored them both. This junior doctor was actually advocating Edwina's release because staying in hospital was the least safest option for her?

He gathered his papers, shook their hands and said earnestly, "Move her ASAP," and walked away through the swing doors.

Picking up their coats and bags, they slipped quietly out of the ward. Visiting wasn't until 2 pm, so they had agreed in advance to find a café and discuss the options once the doctor had finished.

They headed towards the local wine bar. They parked up, walked through the precinct and settled themselves by a roaring log fire, the squishy leather sofas enveloping them.

Vanessa ordered two coffees and two pieces of lemon drizzle cake—she needed sugar and lots of it!

"Ok, so first off, explain all that medical stuff. It's abysmal that he just assumed we'd know what he was saying." Diana bit into her cake and stared hard at Vanessa.

"Well, KUB is an x-ray—kidneys, ureter and bladder. If that's negative, the next logical step is a cystoscopy—a camera into the bladder. It may be that anything suspicious hasn't shown up on the x-ray. They usually do a cystoscopy under a general anaesthetic—well they did in my day—but that might have changed. I should have asked. I'm not sure if she's consented to it. They got her Living Will, so I guess she's decided to allow them to go ahead."

"What about this MRSA thing? Christ, I couldn't believe it when he effectively said she'll die if she stays!"

Vanessa sipped her coffee, thoughtful for a moment.

"Well, she is weak, we know that, and an invasive procedure I guess puts her at greater risk. I was surprised he was so candid about it though."

"If she's not on the operating list till next week, we can't leave her on that ward." Diana pressed on.

"She isn't getting much rest and being surrounded by all the coming and going can't be helping."

"They've got a private wing." Vanessa had already been mulling this over in her mind. "It's not like she can't afford it."

Diana pulled out her mobile and dialled the hospital.

"Hello, could you put me through to the private wing please?"

Whilst on hold, she placed her hand over the mouthpiece. "We're both signatories on her bank account, so we can issue a cheque on her behalf."

Edwina was fastidious about her finances. She had never had an outstanding debt and despite substantial savings, she lived pretty frugally. Both her daughters knew that there was over thirty thousand pounds in her current account alone. Repeatedly over the years, they'd had conversations about how sensible that was (or not in their opinion) but she adamantly kept that balance for 'emergencies.'

It would appear that day had arrived!

Diana was connected to the private wing administrator. She explained the situation that Edwina had funds to pay for her own room and was unable to return home in her current state. The paperwork would need completing and if they met on the ward this afternoon whilst visiting Edwina, it could all be arranged for the following day.

"Right, we're getting somewhere." Diana drained her coffee cup and looked at her sister. "Now, we just need to convince Mummy!"

Chapter 13

They arrived on the ward bang on two o'clock. Edwina's curtain was drawn around her bed and they tentatively peaked behind it. She was asleep…or was she dead?

Her mouth was slack. Her hair wildly across her pillow and because her teeth weren't in situ, her cheeks had sunk into her face, giving her a skeletal look. She twitched.

Not dead then!

They let out a small sigh and collared two plastic chairs, sitting themselves alongside her bed. It was difficult to understand why two visitors were allowed for each patient but in reality, there wasn't enough room to comfortably sit without chair backs clashing together with neighbouring visitors. The gentleman alongside Edwina wasn't blessed this afternoon with visitors, so the two sisters sat and chatted about nothing in particular, waiting for Edwina to stir.

She didn't.

Time was ticking by and the nice lady from the private wing was due at 2:30. They'd been hoping to explain to Edwina the rationale for moving her before the paperwork needed signing.

After fifteen minutes, Diana stroked Edwina's hand.

Nothing.

More insistently she shook it saying, "Mummy," in a calm but determined voice.

Gradually Edwina stirred and opened her eyes. "Hello, darling," she said, making no effort to move. Her daughters smiled at her.

"How are you feeling today?" Vanessa asked, absently straightening her thin blanket. "Tired, I'm absolutely jiggered." *Good,* they thought, *she's being sensible and honest today.*

"I spent all day yesterday in the garden and I'm paying the price today."

Okay, scrub the sensible, thought Diana.

Nothing to do with the fact you were threatening all and sundry with your 'fucking stick' last night, thought Vanessa.

"You look pretty exhausted. Look, we had a chat with the doctor this morning and they want to do a few more tests to find out why you are so tired. But they know how noisy it is on this ward."

"Oh, it is," Edwina interjected. "There's stuff happening all the time. Some old lady was yelling and swearing last night, demanding to go home. Poor old soul. But I couldn't get to sleep with all the racket."

The temptation to respond 'that was you' was almost overwhelming, but Diana carried on with her theme.

"Precisely, so they are going to move you for a bit of peace and quiet. A nice room on the private wing, your own bathroom. You can watch the snooker on TV and sleep undisturbed."

Edwina looked at her.

"Oh, that would be lovely. Will Daddy come to visit?"

This repeated reference to their departed father was distressing but it was obviously providing Edwina with some much-needed comfort.

"I'm not sure, he's very busy, but you know he would want you to have the very best."

Vanessa knew that any mention of something their father approved of was a sure-fire way of getting their mother on side.

At that moment, a middle-aged lady appeared in a blue skirt and jacket with a tasteful floral blouse. Her badge said Marjorie Jacob, Administrator, Nightingale Wing. She held out a hand to Edwina, introducing herself and acknowledging, with a not unfriendly nod, the two visitors.

She explained that the papers needed signing, double checked all the information, including most importantly her bank details.

"I've got my cheque book here." Edwina grasped her handbag, frantically searching for through the contents.

"It's ok, Mummy, I've got it here."

"Why?" Her mother's retort was short and suspicious.

"You wanted it kept safe. I said I'd keep it for you," Diana replied.

"Oh, oh yes, right." Edwina didn't sound convinced but then again, she didn't want anyone running off with it.

Diana had made out the cheque to the Nightingale Wing. It was for seven nights, the minimum they'd accept, but given she was probably going to be in hospital for at least that long, both her daughters thought it was a price worth paying.

"You do understand this is just for the room. The treatment remains on the NHS."

Marjorie reiterated.

"Yes, and she can be moved later today?" Vanessa asked hopefully.

"Well, if not today, then first thing tomorrow. We're waiting on a discharge."

Diana passed the pen to her mother to sign the cheque.

"I don't have my glasses, where do I sign?"

Her daughter held her pen over the signature line and Edwina feebly attempted to write her name. She always signed her name in full—Edwina I Thompson. Clear, upright letters, no fancy flourishes or curly patterns. Today, she struggled. Her immaculate penmanship failed her.

What looked like a drunken spider missing a couple of limbs had traversed the signature line. It was her name but it was doubtful it would pass close inspection at the bank.

Diana handed the cheque to Marjorie as Edwina collapsed back on her pillows, exhausted by her efforts.

A tear off receipt was offered and Diana took this, putting into a folder in her bag with the documentation she thought was needed. It included the cheque book, Living Will copies, bank statements and now the confirmation of payment for the private facilities. As always, Diana was as fastidious as her mother in having documentation in order in case it was needed.

"Well, goodbye, Mrs Thompson, we'll see you later." Another courteous nod and Marjorie was on her way back upstairs to the rarefied atmosphere of the private wards.

"I'm going to rest now." Edwina looked shattered. Their visit had lasted less than an hour, but they acknowledged that today their mother wasn't going to be able to take any more.

Returning the plastic chairs to the side walls, they gathered up their belongings, whispered goodbye to their mother and exited into the early December afternoon.

Both felt relieved that something productive had come out of the day.

They hugged each other goodbye in the car park and went home to their own lives.

Vanessa walked through the door an hour later to be greeted by Simba. Leaping up at her, barking excitedly and running to bring his bedraggled, somewhat smelly, old teddy bear which he deposited at her feet, she laughed at his antics. He danced around her as she poured some milk into his bowl—his favourite treat and probably one that Dan hadn't indulged him in over the last couple of days.

She walked down the garden path to their office annexe, the security light coming on to light the way.

Dan was at his desk, head down, busily working on some sketches for a client. Her early arrival had caught him unawares.

He beamed at his wife. God she looked tired.

"Hello, darling." He rose from his chair and came towards her. "You're early, how's mother?"

She sank into his embrace. She was quite a bit shorter than Dan and her head only came up to the middle of his chest.

"Ok, she was tired so we left early. We're getting her moved to the private wing tomorrow."

"Tell you what, let me just finish this. I'll be fifteen minutes or so. Go and have a soak and I'll get a takeaway ordered. Then we can have a glass of wine and you can fill me in, ok?"

Gratefully, she nodded, looked up, kissed him and ran her hand over his cheek.

"Perfect, everything ok here?"

"Yep, I'll get you up to speed over dinner."

She headed back indoors and taking her overnight bag upstairs, she ran the bath water, properly hot with bubbles. Waiting for the tub to fill, she sat on her bed, Simba lying across looking at her with those big brown eyes, possessed by every Labrador. She stroked his silky ears, buried her face in his fur and let the tears fall. Simba lay still, not fussing but gently licking her hand, just to remind her all would be ok.

After a couple of minutes, she raised her head, kissed him on his head and went into the bathroom for a long, restorative soak.

Chapter 14

Sunday afternoon. Vanessa sat in her squishy sofa, feet tucked under her, enjoying a cup of tea and flicking through her *Good Housekeeping* magazine. The log fire was crackling gently and Simba lay across the front of the fire surround, stretched out, twitching occasionally as he chased something furry in his sleep.

Yesterday had been a full-on day. Caitlin and Sam had finally moved house, so it had been all hands to the pump, humping furniture, hanging curtains and making beds. It had felt great to do something normal. The physical exertions of taking things down two flights of stairs from their flat, loading into the hire van, and then carrying into their little terraced house had meant that both Vanessa and Dan had been properly exhausted at the end of the day. Vanessa had supplied bacon sandwiches and flasks of tea to keep them all going during the day. When they eventually got home as daylight was fading, a soak in the bath, a massive takeaway pizza and a very nice bottle of South African Pinotage had guaranteed a solid night's sleep. It was the first night in two weeks that Vanessa hadn't been playing over the options about Edwina's health in her head. Diana had said she'd cover the Saturday visiting with Michael and allow her sister time to concentrate on Caitlin's move.

Edwina had undergone the cystoscopy on Friday but there was no news, it being the weekend, so they'd agreed to visit together on Monday.

Vanessa and Dan had a lazy Sunday morning, stirring as the winter sun streamed through the bedroom curtains. A dog walk round the local park and rugby fields had provided some much-needed fresh air and they'd strolled hand in hand, catching up on the comings and goings in the business. This wasn't unusual and normally their weekend dog walks and dinner conversations were punctuated by discussions on handling ongoing disputes and differences with tradesmen Dan had to outsource work to. Whilst he had regular contacts that he'd happily vouch for their work, occasionally problems arose with standards of work and Dan was very conscious that his good name was at stake. Vanessa had long ago resigned herself to accepting that running your own business meant you never really got time off but usually, they shared the stresses and strains of the workload and it all turned out ok in the end. She was conscious though that in the last couple of weeks, Dan had been taking on the additional pressures all alone, allowing her to focus on her mother's situation.

Vanessa knew he needed a bit of time to off-load and it felt good to spend some time together talking through the ongoing projects and concentrating on something other than Edwina and her situation.

Intermittently over the years, they'd considered their retirement options and how they'd either sell or wind up the business when the time came. Sensing Dan's frustrations with the current position, Vanessa made, what she felt was a valid point.

"I'm not sure it's worth all the hassle continuing with this. If I've learned nothing else recently, it's life is too short to waste doing stuff we don't enjoy."

Dan looked a bit alarmed. He was fed up dealing with petty issues in the business but that didn't mean he wanted to jack it all in! The rest of the work he loved. Doing business gave him a huge buzz. He looked at his wife. She was tired but it was difficult to judge whether this was down to Edwina's current state or she was just at the end of her tether with the business.

"Let's not be hasty, we can talk it through when things are more settled with mother."

Vanessa nodded and he realised she was once again distracted by thought of hospitals and his mother-in-law's long-term care.

Good, he thought, *let's park discussions about jacking in the business, at least for the moment.*

Now, sitting in front of the fire, Vanessa's eyes started to close. The December afternoon was drawing in and the white twinkling lights off the Christmas tree, situated in the corner of the room, were mesmerising.

Vanessa LOVED Christmas. All the preparations, shopping, wrapping, cooking. Others bemoaned the extra work but she had always revelled in the additional work and her most favourite part was decorating the tree. True, it was artificial but she'd persuaded Dan to buy a really decent one a few years ago and even to his eyes, it was very realistic. Every year, they bought a bauble for the kids (and Simba) and she took delight in unwrapping them and remembering family

Christmas' past. She was also thrilled the second day in January to dismantle it and put it all away again.

This afternoon, it had only been up for a couple of days and she revelled in the tranquillity those little sparkling lights brought to their living room.

She was working through what presents still needed wrapping and any last-minute Amazon orders she might need to arrange when the phone rang. She saw Diana's name on the call list and clicked the answer button.

"Hiya, good timing, I'm enjoying the fireside and remains of a glass of red. How goes your Sunday?"

Diana was making strange hiccupping sounds down the phone and her sister realised she was crying.

"What is it? What's happened?"

"It's c...c...cancer." Diana stammered out. "She's got bladder cancer," and then gave vent to full on sobbing.

Vanessa waited, making soothing noises, until the storm of Diana's upset had started to abate.

In truth, she wasn't that surprised. Having witnessed the amount of blood her mother was passing, Vanessa knew it indicated there was something more serious than a urine infection. As Diana regained some composure, Vanessa was able to garner some more information from her.

"Mummy called this morning. That was a surprise as she obviously remembered our phone number! Anyhow, she was chatting quite normally, you know, weather, Mark and Ruth, Christmas and then just out of the blue says 'so a bit of a bugger about this cancer, not sure where I caught it from!' Then she just carried on talking about the house and buying Christmas cards. I said, hang on, what have they said about cancer and she replied, oh, the doctor came this morning and said it's in my bladder. They're coming tomorrow to talk about surgery."

With that, Diana started crying again, though more controlled this time.

"She was just so matter of fact. I don't think she really understands. And she's all alone in that room, and there's no one for her to talk to, and she just seems to have accepted it. And that doctor said she'd die in there if we didn't get her out. We need to get her out. But she's not well enough to go home and who knows how long she's got. And she can't have surgery, she's too weak and that'd kill her."

Eventually, Diana paused for breath.

"Ok, well the good news is she seems to be taking it in her stride. I'll come down first thing and we'll try and speak with the doctors and get a clear picture. We may need to look at home nursing or a nursing home, but we can discuss that tomorrow."

Vanessa's calm, matter of fact tone, got through to her sister. Whilst Vanessa was as distressed by the news as Diana, she knew that for now, she needed to present a strong, practical focus for them both.

"Let's do a bit of googling this afternoon for local nursing homes and we can compare notes tomorrow. I'll pick you up first thing and we can then just sit and wait until the doctors arrive. You ok now?"

"Yes, thanks, I'm sorry. It was just the way she blurted it out mixed in with everything else. I just needed to process it. You ok? How did the move go?"

They chatted for a few minutes more about family stuff and then Diana said quietly, "I'll see you tomorrow. Thanks, I couldn't do this without you."

"We'll get through it together. Have a good evening and I'll see you in the morning."

Vanessa put the phone down and Dan looked quizzically at her.

"It's cancer," was all she said as the tears quietly slipped over her cheeks.

Chapter 15

Edwina surveyed the people clustered round her bed. The very tall doctor stood at the foot, notes in hand. He had a kindly face but was little more than a boy! No tie she noticed. She didn't approve. A nicely turned-out man in a suit commanded respect. James would have something to say about it when she saw him later. There's no way he'd let the members of his ship turn up looking anything but bandbox smart!

The nurse alongside him was in a dark blue uniform. Matron, Edwina assumed. She had a less kindly face and was fixing her gaze on the patient. Edwina stared back, defiantly. She wasn't going to be intimidated by the 'staff.'

Edwina was tired. She wanted to sleep. They just wouldn't stop talking. She tried very hard to concentrate on what they were saying but it was utterly exhausting. Vanessa was quiet, though Diana's tone was becoming more strident. Goodness, she had a sharp way about her that one. She was given the doctor a piece of her mind and no mistake.

Mr Christopher Curry was a Special Surgical Registrar attached to the Urology Unit. Contrary to Edwina's assertion, he was in his early forties. A handsome man of South African descent, with bleach blond hair and a twinkle in his eye, his 6ft 4" frame dominated the room but he was quietly spoken and not intimidating in the way that many people in authority can be.

He was holding the steely gaze of Mrs Thompson's older daughter. He'd explained the biopsy had shown invasive bladder cancer. He kept the language simple though these two were obviously articulate women. It didn't change the fact he was effectively telling them their mother was going to die and whilst it wasn't a great surprise given her age, he knew families invariably found it difficult to process the information when presented with the inevitable. He'd laid out clearly that the only treatment available was to remove Edwina's bladder.

"A cystectomy?" Vanessa had stated.

"Yes." The younger woman obviously had some knowledge.

Diana moved towards the end of the bed. She said in a somewhat urgent manner "You do know she has a Living Will?" They'd already established at the start of the meeting that both sisters had shared Powers of Attorney responsibility for health and well-being as well as Edwina's finances.

Their apparent lack of knowledge about the Living Will was the reason behind Diana's tone. Having issued multiple copies to A&E staff and the private wing administrator and receptionist over the last few days, she couldn't believe the surgeon was unaware of its existence.

"Er, no," he replied somewhat perplexed, flicking through the notes. He looked at the nursing sister and raised a quizzical eyebrow.

"We should have been given a copy of that," the sister said somewhat tartly.

"You have at least four copies that we've provided in the last 48 hours," Vanessa replied just as tartly.

"It's not here in her notes. This does change our approach." Mr Curry was obviously anxious to do the right thing by Edwina, but was also anxious to avoid any contentious complaints from the family.

Diana sat on her mother's bed and took her hand. Gently explaining to her that they had the option of surgery, Edwina attentively listened. Both Diana and Vanessa knew their mother was renowned for believing what 'authority' figures said, so before she gave her time to respond, Diana continued on, saying the decision was Edwina's but she needed to fully understand all her options.

Shrewdly, the old lady looked at the doctor. She assessed the information she'd been given. Firmly but quietly, she spoke.

"So, if I have this operation, I'll be better and can go home?" That was the end goal after all.

"Well, you'd need to have some additional therapy. Either chemotherapy or radiotherapy—we would decide the best option after surgery."

Edwina eyed him sharply.

"What are the risks?" Vanessa spoke from her chair in the corner.

"The usual," countered the staff nurse at the same time that Christopher Curry responded, "It depends."

He looked sideways at his medical companion with something akin to annoyance, thought Vanessa.

"Mrs Thompson, there's always a risk with surgery. But with your recent infections and poor health, and being in an older age bracket, there's the possibility of a stroke or heart attack and of course, post-operative infection is highly possible, especially as you'll need a catheter in place."

Edwina considered. She wanted to go home. It sounded like that wasn't an option any time soon if she had surgery. She also thought about her mother, Grace. She'd died of breast cancer in the early 1970s. She'd had radiotherapy at the Royal Marsden Hospital. Edwina, an only child, remembered walking those long, disinfectant filled hospital corridors to visit the skeletal form of her beloved mother. Sunken eyes, papery thin-skinned hands—a living corpse. She didn't need that.

She sighed and looked at her children who were uncharacteristically quiet.

Both Vanessa and Diana were honourable women. Whilst they had the power to make decisions on her behalf, whilst she was still able, the choice must be Edwina's. They were here to speak on her behalf, put across her wishes if she was unable to do so, but they would not make the decision for her if she was capable.

"What do you think, girls?"

Vanessa looked straight at her mother.

"It's for you to decide, Mummy, and we'll support you whatever you decide. You have always said you don't want to be a 'cabbage' and there is a risk of that with a stroke."

The nursing sister took in a breath and went to speak but Vanessa stilled her with a raised hand, but never took her eyes off her mother.

"But, you have to understand that if you choose not to have the surgery, there can be only one outcome."

She stopped, and Edwina inclined her head slightly, indicating she had taken all on board.

Fixing her deep brown eyes on Mr Curry, Edwina took a breath.

"Thank you, doctor. On consideration, I really don't want all that pulling about. How long have I got?"

Her matter-of-fact tone took Christopher Curry by surprise but he had an admiration for the old girl and could see where her daughters got their common-sense from. This was often a conversation with family that was traumatic for all concerned, but they were all being pragmatic and sensible in their thought processes.

"Hard to say without having a look inside and getting some samples, but I'd say 6–12 months."

Vanessa kept her eyes downcast. Diana fixed her eyes on her mother's contemplative face.

Twelve months, thought Edwina. *I can go home, tend the garden, enjoy one more summer, put my affairs in order and then just fade away.*

"Lovely," she said. "Many thanks but I'll just go home and let nature take its course."

Vanessa let out a long breath she wasn't aware she'd been holding. You can't be surprised that your ninety something mother is drawing to her end of life but you can hope it isn't filled with pain, loss of dignity and hospital beds.

Mr Curry nodded.

"Very well, Mrs Thompson, it's your decision and we will obviously honour that. I'll need you to sign some papers just explaining that you understand what we've discussed. You still need a few days to recuperate from the biopsy but we'll get you out of here by Christmas. If I may?" He gestured to the door. "I'll go through everything with your daughters. Nurse, a cup of tea for Mrs Thompson, I think."

He shook Edwina's hand and she noticed his firm grip.

"A pleasure and I'm sorry it wasn't better news. We'll keep an eye on you at regular intervals."

"Lovely," Edwina said again and relaxed back into her pillows. *Home soon,* she thought.

She'd have to fill James in later when she saw him.

Diana and Vanessa exited through the door after the surgeon and followed him down the royal blue carpeted corridor. Not for the first time, Diana wondered how they kept it clean what with trolleys, commodes and the like trundling up and down. He gestured to them to have a seat in the leatherette armchairs in the waiting area. It was quiet. Few patients were here with Christmas only a few days away.

"First off, let me apologise again for the lack of information on the Living Will. Admin cock-up. Not unusual but I'm glad you were here to raise it."

Diana acknowledged his apology and said she'd hand over yet another copy to the nursing station to go into Edwina's urology notes.

"She can't go home yet. She really is too weak. We'll be shutting the private wing in a couple of days for Christmas and I'd like to avoid putting her back on the wards."

"I guess she could come to us," Diana said. Working through in her mind how Edwina would cope with their stairs and their Christmas guests, Christopher's voice cut through her thoughts.

"Not a good idea—she still needs nursing care. Her catheter is still in and we need to keep an eye on her bloods and urine checks. I'd suggest a nursing home for a bit. Sorry, bit presumptuous but I'm assuming she could afford it?"

"We've thought about the options but you can tell she desperate is to get home. She has the funds for care. Would a private live-in nurse work?"

"Eventually, maybe, but I'd say for the next few weeks, get her into a care home that specialises in end-of-life care too. We really don't know how invasive the cancer is and without opening her up to get a clearer picture of the grade of cancer, we honestly can't tell. My advice, tell her it's a convalescent home. Ladies her age can relate to that. They'd go there after their babies were born. It won't seem such a final step which, frankly, is what it may end up being."

They talked some more about the options and processes and he said they'd send a clinic appointment for next month to review her with the Consultant Urologist. Mr Curry mentioned her ongoing shoulder pain may in fact be secondary bone cancer depending on whether the cancer had spread and he'd like to get her scanned before she left so they'd have a better idea of the overall picture.

After he left them, both women sat sipping some tepid watery coffee brought by the receptionist. They made plans to go back to Diana's and starting ringing the various nursing homes they'd short-listed the night before. Good old Google—they had four local options including a brand-new facility literally at the end of Diana's road. She thought this could be really convenient but Vanessa worried it would be too close for them both.

Picking up their coats and bags, they went back up the corridor to Edwina's room. They'd have half an hour with her and then leave her to rest whilst they focused on getting her a place to stay over Christmas.

"Blimey," said Diana, "let's hope we don't get 'there is no room at the Inn' response." Chuckling at her sister's dark humour, Vanessa linked her arm in Diana's and they sallied forth towards Edwina's room.

Chapter 16

The air was filled with the aroma of boiled cabbage and wee. This was the first home on their list and only ten minutes from Diana's house. The dual carriageway alongside the muddy patch of what passed for a front garden kept up a constant hum of traffic with the intermittent thunderous rumble of large industrial lorries making their way along the coast towards Brighton.

Having been admitted through the entry system which Vanessa privately felt was more like an HM Prison, they'd been ushered towards two leatherette chairs in the hallway.

There were fifteen residents crammed into the small area, all shuffling and queuing towards a small Perspex window. Behind this sat a young woman doling out cash to each resident.

"Come on, Stan, come and get your spends."

A gentleman who was of indeterminate age, though probably around eighty, stepped forward. He had little of his white hair left but was dressed in a pair of grey trousers, hanging loosely from his frame. A woollen waistcoat was over his checked flannelette shirt and the remnants of his lunch dotted his tartan tie. He wore plaid slippers and a dazed expression.

Taking his 'spends' from the Perspex hole in the wall, he joined the line of his compatriots as they waited for the minibus to pull up outside.

Vanessa caught his eye and smiled whilst Diana gave a cheery, "Good afternoon."

He looked blankly at them both with watery pale blue eyes but didn't either register or react to their greeting.

"Come on, you lot, let's be 'aving yer."

A large man appeared in the entrance door sporting a suit jacket that strained against his upper arms and whose belly was barely contained by a blue shirt, buttons ready to pop at any time. He had what looked like a tub of Brylcream slicking down his thinning hair and was chivvying the rabble along.

"Christmas lights are awaiting, move along now. Dave's the name, and bussing's the game."

A small lady in an oversized coat passed by. She wore a scarf tied under her frail chin and was assisted by a stick in each hand.

"We're going to see the Christmas lights and have mince pies," she informed Diana and Vanessa.

"And we're allowed to spend some of our pocket money!" Vanessa smiled.

"Lovely, have a wonderful time. Good you're wrapped up, it's chilly out there," Diana responded.

"Doris, come along, stop your nattering," commanded Dave, the driver.

Rolling his eyes heavenward at Diana and Vanessa to indicate he didn't have the time to hang around, he took the handles of a wheelchair from one of the care assistants.

The occupant was a man, again in his eighties or early nineties with a blanket over his knees and a flat cap on his head.

"GOODBYE, ARTHUR, BE A GOOD BOY," the care assistant shouted at him as he was handed over. He looked hard at her and gave a slight inclination of his head. Whatever his condition or age, by no means did he appreciate being called 'a boy!'

Diana thought, *I wonder what his story is? Does he have a family? What was his profession? Did he serve in the war?*

As the sorry little troop headed out for their afternoon of freedom, the two sisters looked at each other and Vanessa pulled a face. It basically said 'we can't put Mummy here,' but at that moment, the home manager appeared.

She was a small, dark-haired lady wearing a black suit and sensible flat shoes. Her face had a severe countenance, probably not helped by the fact her hair was pulled into a tight bun.

Behind the Perspex window, the care assistant and her colleague were talking about a couple of the residents and were loud enough to be heard in the hallway.

"If they get Rosie there and back without pissing herself, it'll be a good day."

The manager gave some sort of clicking noise as she passed and a look passed between her and her staff. It wasn't a reprimand as such, but both carers lowered their voices and slid the plastic window shut.

"My apologies," the manager said, extending her hand to both Diana and Vanessa. Her accent, they guessed it to be Spanish or Italian, sounded quite harsh.

"Our rezidents are off for an outing, so it's been a leetle bizzy. Shall we walk? I'm Mrs Vilson."

"Not a problem, and thank you for seeing us."

They collected their things and headed down a corridor. Diana supposed Mrs 'Vilson' had married an English Mr Wilson.

"Let uz go to zee lounge."

There was a room at the end of the hallway. To be fair, it was light and large but the aroma of cabbage was stronger in here. Big picture windows filled one wall and there were some patio doors at one end that led onto a green space. To call it a garden would have been an exaggeration. There were some old cardboard boxes piled up, soggy from the rain, which looked like they'd once held clinical wipes and paper towels. An empty bird feeder hung sadly from a tree. No contents enticed feathered visitors and Diana spied a plastic green rat trap box at the bottom of the lichen covered fence.

Chairs were placed around the three sides of the walls, cheek by jowl with one another. They looked like soldiers lined up, all regimented and in a dull green colour. Some were covered with crocheted seat cushions, others had what were obviously waterproof covers to avoid the likes of Rosie from pissing on them!

In one corner sat a wizened old lady. Wearing a cardigan about four sizes too big for her, old slippers and a checked skirt, she appeared to be enveloped by her seat. Sitting at an awkward angle, feet resting on the Zimmer frame in front of her, she was evidently asleep—or was she dead thought Diana. Mouth agape, no teeth and no obvious movement, they were both transfixed. Mrs 'Vilson' was intoning on about the facilities and seemed oblivious to the sleeping/dead resident.

"Let's look at a room," she continued and marched off down a side corridor.

They passed rooms with sleeping occupants, some were staring out of their window and one was talking animatedly to a toy monkey she had on her lap. Cradling the stuffed animal like a baby, she was content to nuzzle it like a sleeping child, transfixed by her charge and ignoring the passing visitors.

The room they entered was small, contained a bed, small bedside table, chair and commode. There was an adjustable bed table, similar to those in hospital, that can be moved up and down in height to allow patients to eat whilst confined to bed. The table contained the remains of lunch—a congealed meat of indeterminate origin, boiled cabbage and potatoes and some form of sponge pudding and custard.

Mrs 'Vilson' clicked her tongue again and as an orderly was passing, snapped her fingers, causing them to halt in the doorway.

"Clear this away," she instructed. There was obvious annoyance in her tone but Diana and Vanessa registered she had neither used the staff member's name or added a please or thank you.

Both had seen enough. There was no way Edwina was staying here.

"We take people from the local authority, but we have fee paying residents too."

"Well, thank you for showing us round, we really appreciate it," said Diana, taking charge.

"We're obviously in the very early stages of looking but we'll let our mother have all the information and get back in touch if we need anything else. Thank you so much for your time, especially when you are so busy."

Vanessa hid a smile. There were times when Diana sounded just like Edwina—be polite, be authoritative and get out as fast as possible.

Shaking Mrs Vilson's hand once again, they exited the double doors and headed to the car park.

Fixing their seatbelts in place, they looked at one another with a mix of amusement and horror.

"Fucking hell, I think we can definitely scrub that one off the list of possibles," said Diana. "I know it's only early afternoon but shall we find a pub?"

"Good idea, and I think we need to narrow our search to private paying places from now on."

Putting the car into first gear, Diana eased out onto the dual carriageway and they headed towards the local wine bar to regroup and re-assess their options.

Chapter 17

Edwina rested her eyes, sitting in the winged back armchair of her new abode.

Sunset House was a large nursing home set in a tree lined avenue. Her room, whilst small, was cosy and overlooked the driveway and entrance porch so she had a steady stream of people coming and going that she could watch.

It had been a busy few days. Diana and Vanessa had explained the doctors said she needed to convalesce before going home and they'd found this lovely old fashioned Edwardian home. It had lots of facilities, including an active residents' diary with everything from craft sessions, singalongs, bingo and film afternoons.

Of course, Edwina wasn't really interested in those things, though she'd heard they had a regular visit from a lady with a black Labrador and she'd certainly be up for that.

Edwina knew she was having to pay for her stay but as both girls had pointed out, she had the money and it is what James would want. She was exceptionally tired. Her shoulder hurt and the journey this morning from the hospital had been fairly traumatic.

Having secured the room for Edwina at Sunset House, both her daughters had felt relieved. It had a lovely feel with friendly staff, a beautiful garden and a large, airy (non-cabbage smelling) dining room, complete with fish tank and minibar!

Her room, whilst not large, was all they had for the next month and it had a basin and sink but no en-suite. However, with her catheter still in situ they felt this was a price worth paying, literally. Two weeks 'rent' up front had sealed the deal.

Edwina had been surprisingly compliant to the idea of not going home immediately, though it was still her long-term aim.

In order to personalise her new space, they'd been to the bungalow the previous day. Having updated the neighbours on the plans, they found some nightdresses and a spare pair of slippers. They also put together a few skirts and blouses that could easily be used without hurting her shoulder and some plain cardigans for warmth. Included in her overnight bag was her favourite picture of James, taken when he was a naval apprentice in the early 1940s, her favourite cushion with Labrador tapestry front and a couple of photos of Vanessa, Diana, Dan and Michael from one of their joint holidays. They'd included her regular talc—Lacome by Coty, some stockings (Edwina refused to contemplate ever wearing tights) and her address book. Diana had got a small arrangement of yellow roses and freesias—Edwina's favourite flowers—for her bedroom windowsill and Vanessa had bought a *Woman's Own* and *People's Friend* magazines together with a crossword book.

They'd arrived at the hospital and waited for two hours for a porter to take Edwina downstairs to the entrance. She was in her nightdress and dressing gown, being too weak to get dressed. There was talk of an ambulance transfer but the receptionist at the private wing desk said it was an unknown timeslot as there were so many being discharged today. Christmas was two days away and the private wards were closing, and the main hospital wards were getting rid of as many as possible before the festive season truly got going. Edwina was the last one on her floor to leave and there was an eery silence about the place.

In the end, as she was getting increasingly fractious, they decided to take her to Sunset House themselves in Diana's car. It was only ten minutes from the hospital and this hanging around was getting to all of them.

Sourcing a wheelchair, they manoeuvred her into the lift and down to the entrance. Diana was challenged driving the chair.

"Bloody hell, it's like a supermarket trolley, it's got a mind of its own." Even Edwina giggled as she was bundled into the lift.

Weaving in and out of the ongoing hordes of visitors arriving at the hospital, they'd eventually made it to the entrance. Diana went to get the car whilst Vanessa stayed with their mother, close to the doorway.

It was blowing a gale, huge swirling winds gusted past, trees swaying on the edge of the car park and litter being sucked from the overflowing bins, casting disposable coffee cups and sandwich wrapping into the wind, mixing with the leaf remnants from the trees and depositing them in untidy bundles by the doorway. The wind was bitter and every time someone passed by the automatic doors, it whipped into the entrance way. Vanessa had tucked her fake fur lined coat around Edwina to provide some warmth. She was wrapped in her fleecy dressing gown, but having been in hospital for nearly a month, she was definitely more frail than either of her girls had seen her before. She also had a wide-eyed look as if she was baffled by the noise and hubbub of the hospital environment.

The entrance was reserved for ambulance drop offs but both women had decided that there was no way they could push Edwina to the car park, so Diana would just pull up and they'd be gone quickly. They were both anxious enough to not stand for any little administrative Hitler to challenge them on their use of the space and were ready to defend their right to park if anyone said anything.

Vanessa saw her sister's red Ka pull up at the end of the roadway to the front door. If they'd known they were going to act as hospital transport they might have bought one of the other bigger cars, but thinking their mother was going via ambulance, they'd only brought the little two door with them.

"Here we go," Vanessa said to Edwina as she heaved on the wheelchair handles. "We'll be as quick as we can," and with that, she launched them into the swirling wind, tucking her head down and pushing the chair with all her strength.

As she approached the car, a young nurse came up to her. "Want a hand?"

"Oh, bless you, thanks. She's got a catheter in and has a bad shoulder so I'm a bit anxious moving her."

"No worries, let's get you sorted, lovely." The nurse bent to Edwina who looked bemused and befuddled.

Diana got out of the car. Vanessa shouted to her over the wind, "You get back in, she might need pulling across if she can't swing round."

They managed to get Edwina onto her feet but conscious that her mother was now exposed to the winter winds, Vanessa said to her, "Right, Mummy, just sit yourself down and I'll swing your legs in."

She'd had the forethought to put a plastic bag on the passenger seat which would make it easier to swivel Edwina in.

"Mind my arm," her mother warned, but her voice was swallowed by the winter wind. She was obviously anxious of any pain.

Rather inelegantly, they got her sitting down and with a mix of pulling, pushing, twisting and slithering, eventually got Edwina facing forwards with her feet in the footwell.

Reaching in, Vanessa tried to pass the seatbelt across for Diana to lock it in place, but moving Edwina's arm to try and slot it through caused her to scream out in pain. "Sod it," said Vanessa, "we're not going far, we'll risk it."

Thanking the nurse profusely for her help and her offer to return the wheelchair, Vanessa quickly loaded Edwina's hospital bag into the boot. "Where's my bag?" Edwina frantically asked.

"It's ok, it's in the back," Diana reassured her. "Where's my stick?"

"IT'S IN THE BACK," Diana retorted. She was getting stressed and sounded snappish and waspy.

Edwina looked bewildered and Diana immediately felt guilty. Patting her mother's hand, she softened.

"Nessa's got it all sorted, don't worry. We know where everything is. Let's put the heating up a bit, you're frozen."

Vanessa launched herself into the back seat of the car. Diana, who'd got out to allow her sister to climb in, slammed her door and shoved the car into first gear, weaving her way out of the ambulance bay.

That had been a couple of hours ago. After getting Edwina out of the car at Sunset House with help from a couple of orderlies who had been so welcoming, they'd got her settled into her room.

The sisters had agreed with the manager that they'd leave Edwina to get settled and they'd been advised not to visit for a couple of days to allow her to get used to the new surroundings.

The orderly had brought Edwina a cup of tea—she approved, it wasn't in a mug but a nice China cup—and they asked if she'd like a late lunch. She declined, the exertions of the day proving too much for her. She had chosen a ham sandwich and ice cream for her tea and chuckled when they asked if she'd like a sherry with it.

"Thank you, maybe another day," she'd replied.

Diana and Vanessa had offered to unpack her things and toiletries but she said she'd do it herself. She'd been delighted with the photo of James and her favourite cushion and had leant over to smell the arrangement of flowers in her window.

"My girls are so good," she'd said to the staff nurse who introduced herself as Karen. She wanted to take a history and have a chat, so Diana and Vanessa had taken that as an opportunity to kiss their mother goodbye and they'd see her soon.

Exiting the building as the winter sun was setting, they waved to her as she looked out of her window. The old lady looked shattered and they both wondered if this place would be Edwina's final home.

Chapter 18

"But I want to go home. You can't stop me!"

Edwina looked fiercely at the charge nurse who met her gaze with an infuriating detachment.

She'd been in the nursing home a month. Christmas had passed pleasantly enough. Fortunately, she'd been too weak to be forced to join in all the jollity though she'd had a visit from Santa on Christmas Eve afternoon. He'd left a present of some cheap bubble bath which she'd shoved in the back of the wardrobe.

She'd suffered the indignity of some chap coming along to 'wash her bottom.' He'd been very matter of fact about it but she'd already decided she'd take care of her own personal hygiene from now on, thank you very much.

Diana had popped in with Michael on Christmas Day for an hour but she was still very tired from the hospital transfer and had been relieved when they left, though it had been lovely to see them and they'd brought her Christmas cards to read. Vanessa had sent cards on her behalf to all her friends updating them on the situation, so most knew she'd been unwell and had sent good wishes to her for a speedy recovery. Having a regular diet of fresh food and veg for the last four weeks, not to mention the daily tablets (which she'd sometimes forgotten at home), she was stronger than she'd been in months.

So, she was ready to go home!

But everyone kept avoiding the subject. She was well aware that they were placating her with 'soon' and 'not long' but there wasn't any progress being made. "Would you like a cup of tea?"

The charge nurse was bundling up some washing to go to the laundry.

That was another annoyance—they just kept taking her things to 'wash and freshen up.' She wasn't an invalid and she didn't need anyone doing her washing. She spent some evenings using the small sink in her room to wash out her stockings and underwear. There wasn't any soap powder but she had her Pears soap in her sponge bag, and many a time in the war (and quite often since), she had washed her clothes with a sturdy bar of soap. The girls always laughed when they first went abroad on holiday in 1974 and Edwina had spent an afternoon at the Tenerife Hotel washing everyone's smalls and hanging them discreetly on the 15th-floor balcony to dry in the summer heat. James had taken the girls swimming in the hotel pool to give her a chance to do the laundry—he'd tried to persuade her to use the hotel's own service, but she told him it was money down the drain when she could do it herself.

She looked at the charge nurse with pursed lips.

"No, I do not want a cup of tea." She added a begrudging 'thank you' at the end of the sentence—no need to forget your manners, Edwina.

She looked resignedly out of her window and saw Vanessa and Dan waiting outside for someone to answer the intercom. Grabbing her stick, she immediately left her room, turning right and heading for reception. The woman on the desk, Moira, had let them in and they were signing the visitors' book.

"About time, I'm ready to leave. I'll go and pack."

Both Dan and Vanessa looked taken aback, both by her statement and the ferocity with which it was delivered.

Gently taking her mother's elbow, Vanessa propelled her back towards her room. "Well, aren't you looking spritely today?"

"I'm much better, I need to get home."

They went back into Edwina's room, though she was starting to see it as a prison cell. She sat in the wing back chair in the window alcove, suddenly aware that she was feeling pretty worn out.

Dan sat on the end of her bed, whilst Vanessa pulled another chair up towards her mother's. The television was on—Countdown—but there wasn't any sound. "What's wrong with the television?" Dan asked.

"Mmm? Oh, I don't know, it comes and goes. I have the writing on the screen at home, but they don't have it here."

"You mean subtitles? I'm sure we can find that for you."

Dan's dislike of hospitals also stretched to nursing homes, he realised. Conversations were stilted and false. Given the chance to do something practical, he jumped at the opportunity, picking up the remote controls and flicking through the set-up options.

Chatting to his mother-in-law, Vanessa quietly said, "Just popping to the loo," and went back to reception.

The nursing manager Sue and Senior Nurse Daisy, were talking by the desk. They both smiled at Vanessa as she approached.

"Can I have a quick word?"

"Of course, what can we do for you?"

Sue was a buxom blonde lady, kind face but a steely determination that brooked no nonsense from staff or residents.

"I just wanted a word about Mummy. She's obviously desperate to get home and she does seem better. Is it something we should be looking at?"

"Edwina is certainly a bit stronger physically, but that may just be down to regular eating and medication. She does still get very confused and we need to remember she is terminally ill. She's been tipping the staff again too."

A couple of weeks back, the manager had told Diana that the money Edwina had in her purse was being used to tip the 'hotel' staff who bring her room service and clean her room! The evening staff were worried they'd be accused of taking her money.

Edwina had become anxious and distressed just after Christmas that she had no money to go shopping. Despite explaining, she had no need to go shopping, her levels of anxiety had only increased, so her daughters had put £50 in her purse. It had contented her enough to calm down, but now she had been using that to tip the staff.

They'd all agreed to play along and any time Edwina gave them money, it went straight into the night safe until it could be given back to Vanessa or Diana, who in turn replaced it in Edwina's purse.

It was farcical and Diana found it difficult to maintain this deception with her mother but Vanessa persuaded her that no one was being hurt and it kept Edwina happy.

"She's becoming quite secretive too," went on Sue.

"She is adamant that we don't touch her clothes and things—which is fine—but the other day, she had gone into the day room and the laundry staff returned some nightwear to her drawer. We found a stack of dirty underwear at the back together with some biscuits that had been put out with her afternoon tea. So, whilst physically she's improved, I'm not sure she can cope mentally on her own. That said, we can't keep her here against her will. If she wants to walk out the front door, we can't actually stop her."

This made Vanessa even more anxious.

"We're looking at a live-in nurse but I know she'll resent it and will dismiss them as soon as we've gone. I will talk to her about visiting home for a few hours. That may help."

She made her way back to her mother's room, picking absently at her acrylic nails. As she entered the room, Edwina stopped talking to Dan.

"Hello darling, how are you? What a lovely surprise. This is Daniel, my son-in-law." Dan and Vanessa stared at each other, not sure what to say. She read the 'what the hell?' look on his face, but decided that it was best to ignore her mother's comment.

"It's a lovely day outside, do you fancy a walk round the garden?"

"No, dear, it's full of old people, I'll stay here."

Vanessa didn't dare look at Dan for fear they'd both end up laughing.

They chatted for a while about mundane things—the news, weather, some spring flowers sent by Edwina's sister-in-law, Elizabeth.

"I was thinking, Mummy, if you'd like one day next week, I could come and pick you up and we could pop out for a bite of lunch and maybe call in at the bungalow for a bit to check up on everything?"

Edwina's face broke into a wide smile.

"That would be WONDERFUL. Would you mind, I'd like that very much." Touched by her mother's obvious delight and gratitude, Vanessa bit back tears. "Of course not, I'll see if Di is around and we can have a girls' day out."

"Bless you, darling," Edwina said, holding onto her daughter's hand.

She didn't mention staying or leaving the nursing home so Vanessa felt that it was a stepping stone in the right direction. Maybe they could look to move her back soon.

"It's such a long time since I was home—I've forgotten where things are. Where's the ironing board?"

Dan looked enquiringly at Vanessa. It was an odd statement but she went with it.

"The ironing board is in the hall cupboard, always has been since 1973."

"Oh of course, you're right. The cupboard under the stairs."

Once again Dan and Vanessa looked at each other. "Mother," he said, "you live in a bungalow!"

"Don't be ridiculous," she retorted.

"The house is on three floors. Great nanna and grandpa live on the ground floor, so Mummy and I can have the rest of the house."

Vanessa realised she was talking about her childhood home in South London. Edwina had left in 1947 when she married James. Deciding honesty was the best policy, she said very gently.

"No, Mummy, that was your home before you got married. You've got the bungalow now." Edwina's soft brown eyes looked directly at her daughter.

"I'm sorry, who are you again?"

Chapter 19

Diana had her head in Edwina's fridge, and a pair of yellow rubber gloves on. They'd arrived at their mother's house earlier in the day to have a bit of a clear out now that it looked like Edwina wasn't coming home any time soon. Whilst they'd cleaned the fridge when Edwina went into hospital but every time they visited the house, there was a lingering smell and Diana had decided on a deep disinfectant to tackle it.

Vanessa had spent the morning speaking with an organisation that provided 24-hour live-in nursing care but it was dawning on them that this would not only be astronomically expensive, but there was no way Edwina would agree to it.

They would be on a four-day on, three-day off rotation of two-three nurses. Fair enough, everyone needs time off, but Edwina would be confused with all the coming and going. They would need their own room—tick, not a problem. But they'd need a TV—ok, we can buy another one, and access to the internet. It would need installing as Edwina's bungalow was still stuck in the early 1980s as regards technology, but again, it wasn't insurmountable.

They couldn't stop Edwina going out and about, which was fine but she struggled presently to find her way to and from the toilet, so it might prove more challenging in the longer term. They didn't provide meals—ok, a delivery could be arranged, though Edwina would likely refuse.

More importantly, they weren't able to provide end-of-life care when the time came and both women knew that Edwina would either sack them or make their lives so miserable the nurses would walk out.

"I don't want her to stay at Sunset indefinitely, she wants to come home," Vanessa said. "I know, but we have to face facts—she's still as confused as hell and whilst she gets around with her stick in the home, it's not like here. If she's on her own and forgets the cooker is on, or falls, she could be here for hours, or days, or start a fire, or anything." Diana stuck her head back in the fridge, sniffing.

"Bloody hell, it still smells, what on earth is it? I've even thought of having her to live with us."

Vanessa looked at her sharply.

"You can't do that, you'd kill each other! And to be fair, so would I if she came to us. Let's be honest, she values her independence too much. She's always said about not living in each other's pockets. Remember how she hated it when nanna lived at Edenna?"

Back in the 1960s, before Vanessa's arrival, Edwina and James had built a family home with an interconnecting extension, so Edwina's mother, Grace, could live with them. They've named the house 'Edenna'—a combination of Edwina and the two girls, Jennifer and Diana.

Grace was widowed when Edwina was eighteen months old after her husband, Edwin, had died from wounds in the First World War. She had helped look after the girls when

Edwina had had the opportunity to visit James whilst he was at sea.

Grace was besotted with her grandchildren, but could be jealous of James and Edwina's time together. When he was home on leave, she had a history of making life difficult for her daughter and son-in-law, making the most of having a granny annexe that gave her access to their home at the drop of a hat.

In the end, she had moved out after a major argument, and Edwina had always said that living in such close proximity to her adored mother was more than she could stand. Hence, she had always maintained that she and her own girls should not live cheek by jowl with one another.

Up until now, Edwina's very independent streak had been a god send to her daughters, meaning she was highly capable of taking care of herself despite her advancing years.

"The other thing that worries me," Vanessa went on, "is that if she's here alone and Jennifer finds out, she'll come sniffing round and who knows what she'd get up to or what she'd con her out of."

"Not likely at present—she's still got another two years to serve, and putting it bluntly, I don't think Mummy is going to last that long!"

As she was talking, she suddenly fell back, rocking on her heels.

"Oh, for God's sake!"

The butter dish compartment in the fridge door had been her last place to disinfect and on opening it, a stiff piece of what presumably had one been breaded cod, fell out on the floor beside her. It had a dusky tinge of green from the mould that was attached to it. Holding her rubber gloved wrist to her mouth, Diana looked at her sister in horror.

She leapt to her feet and staggered back a bit towards the kitchen doorway.

"Well, that's the reason for the smell then," Vanessa said. "Come on, give me the gloves, I'll do it."

"That is gross, how long has it been there? No wonder she was bloody ill."

Taking the gloves from her sister, Vanessa gingerly picked up the remnants of the fish and put it in a bin liner, knotting the top as she did so and taking it directly out to the dustbin by the back door.

"I feel sick," said Diana, still shocked that her mother, who was so fastidious about her home, could have had something rotting away in her fridge and not known about it.

Vanessa, giving the door compartment a thorough squirting of disinfectant, chuckling to herself. Out of the two of them, she was the squeamish one but even she could see that Diana was struggling to cope with the find.

Diana put her head in hands.

"Bloody hell, what are we going to do?"

"Let's go and get her and bring her here for the day. We can see how she is when she's here and you never know, it might be what she needs to perk up and resolve things." Vanessa didn't sound convinced by her own argument, but they locked up the bungalow and went to collect their mother for her first return home in six weeks.

Chapter 20

The February sun glinted off the sea in the distance. Edwina, sitting in the front of Vanessa's BMW 5 series was wrapped in a warm coat and gloves with the heated seat on and she marvelled at the sight of the South Downs and Seven Sisters, so close to her heart.

They'd driven along at a pretty sedate pace and Edwina had been thrilled to see the fields overlooking the Channel, populated with fluffy sheep and their expanding waistlines ready for the lambing season in a few weeks.

"Soon be time for some yuvvy yickle yammies," Edwina said.

It was a phrase that apparently their eldest sister Jennifer had coined as a toddler and their mother repeated it every year come spring.

Vanessa gave a sardonic smile to Diana in the rear-view mirror as Diana just shook her head—a mix of exasperation and delight that her mother remembered the phrase.

They didn't speak much—Edwina was evidently enjoying being outside with the different views and as they dropped down towards the Cuckmere Valley with its winding oxbow river heading towards the sea at Birling Gap, Edwina said, "I lost my wedding ring here on a picnic once."

The sisters well knew the story but kept quiet as once more Edwina recounted how the cold water had meant her ring had slipped over her knuckle and it was only good fortune that James had spotted and retrieved it.

They drew up in the driveway of the home that Edwina had lived in for 45 years, 25 of them as a widow, and she breathed an audible sigh of relief.

"Oh look, home," she said quietly.

"I'll come and help you out," Diana said, releasing her seatbelt and opening her rear door. They'd agreed in advance that whilst going in the front door was preferable as it was a shorter distance, there was no way Edwina would be able to navigate the steep step up. Instead they'd go round the pathway to the back door—her usual entrance—which would be easier for her to access.

Stiffly and with some caution, Edwina manoeuvred herself out of the car and leant heavily on Diana's arm. Vanessa had got out and locking the car, had moved to the back door to unlock the house and turn off the security alarm. She also slammed the fridge door shut having given it time to air a bit after 'fish-gate.'

When they'd visited earlier in the day, they'd put the heating on and so, the house was now nice and toasty and welcoming for its returning owner.

"Edwina!" A high-pitched voice echoed down the close and Edith was rushing down, arms wide to envelope her neighbour.

"For fuck's sake," Diana said under her breath, could the woman not give them five minutes.

"How are you? You're looking well. It's lovely to have you back. Are you staying?"

Edwina smiled sweetly but looked a bit bewildered.

"Hello, dear, it's lovely to be home."

"If you don't mind, Edith, we'd like to get Mummy into the warm. It's her first time out." Whilst talking, Diana was gently navigating Edwina and her stick up the garden path. "No worries, I'll give you a hand," said Edith, making towards Edwina's other elbow.

"It's fine, Nessa is here too, so we're all good," Diana retorted, perhaps more strongly than intended, but God, this woman was persistent.

"Oh, ok, I'll pop round later," said Edith.

Diana watched as she hurried down the driveway towards Sandra and Tony's house—no doubt anxious to impart the news of Edwina's return before anyone else did so.

Edwina managed the step into her utility room and through into her kitchen and gave a fulsome, satisfied sigh.

"Come on, let's get you sat down in the lounge and we'll put the kettle on."

Seated in her favourite corner armchair, by the electric fire and resting her head on the high-backed cushions, Edwina closed her eyes and let out a breath of relief. She could see her beloved garden through the lounge window and whilst there wasn't much happening in the February season, it all looked as she'd left it. The house was warm and she smiled to herself as she listened to her daughters chatting in the kitchen, making tea and opening biscuits.

A picture of James in his officer's uniform sat on a coffee table by the French doors. It was similar to the one the girls had brought for her room at Sunset House, but this one had been taken twenty or so years after the first. She smiled to herself—he loved this house and this room in particular. She always felt his presence when she sat here doing her crossword or watching the snooker on television and now, as she relaxed into the chair, looking at his twinkling blue eyes, she felt at peace for the first time in weeks.

Chapter 21

They had agreed that Diana and Vanessa would head into town and get some fish and chips for lunch. Vanessa had suggested to her sister that some breaded cod would be yummy whilst pointedly looking at the fridge. Diana made a face of someone being sick and they both collapsed laughing. Edwina had no idea what they were going on about, but was just pleased to be home and listening to them laughing together.

Both sisters had thought leaving Edwina on her own for a short time would be good. In actual fact, it would be the first time since her admission to hospital in December that she hadn't been around other people.

As they left, she had told them she would put the plates in the oven to warm through and lay the table.

They parked in town and walked to the fish shop, somewhat ironically named Capt. Ahab's. It had been there donkeys years, the main chippy in town and many a family meal had been purchased here. Indeed, Edwina and James had originally used it when they honeymooned here in 1947 and as a family, they'd celebrated the Silver Jubilee in 1977 with fish and chips in the garden. Prior to Diana's first wedding in the early 1980s, they had all feasted on cod and chips for lunch before she got ready to go down the aisle. 'Bit of grease will settle your tum,' their father had stated.

In recent years, they'd used it less, though when Edwina had the grandchildren to stay in the holidays, invariably the post beach meal was in the restaurant attached to the side of the shop.

Having purchased three small cod and one large chips, they returned to the BMW and headed back home. Edwina had been on her own for forty minutes or so which they thought was long enough.

On entering the kitchen, it was baking hot and not from the heating being on.

Edwina, who they could see in the lounge chair, appeared not to have moved. Obviously, she had though as the oven was on full blast and the plates were blistering under the intense heat.

"Shit," said Vanessa, getting a tea towel to remove them and then deciding two towels was a better option.

She lifted the plates onto the hob and turned the oven off.

"We'll have to leave them to cool before we use them," she said turning to her sister who was examining the contents on the kitchen table.

"Did you fancy marmite with your fish?"

Edwina had made an attempt at laying the table. Her old white and green table cloth—darned so much, there was little of the original cloth remaining—and the table mats 'Sights of the Lake District' bought on some long-forgotten holiday, had been laid out. Cutlery was also out but not in any particular order and she had obviously taken the first things out of the larder she could lay her hands on. Alongside the marmite was some marmalade and a tin of peaches.

It reminded Vanessa of when the children had asked when they were younger to help lay the table. They'd made an effort of sorts but didn't want to do it right in case they were asked again.

Replacing the marmalade, marmite and peaches with a jar of ketchup and tartare sauce, Diana went into the lounge to rouse her mother.

She sat in the chair, mouth open but no sound. For a minute Diana wondered if she was dead. Had she made it home in time to collapse quietly in her favourite chair and go gently into that good night?

Edwina's false teeth dropped from her upper jaw to the lower—Diana jumped. Obviously, they were looser than before but the motion had aroused her mother, who breathed deeply and opened her eyes.

She fixed Diana with an icy stare, not recognising her or her surroundings immediately.

"We're back with the food. Would you like a drink with it?"

Coming to gradually, Edwina nodded.

"Squash, tea, Sherry?"

"Sherry."

Diana smiled and went to the drinks cabinet to liberate the Bristol cream that had been gathering dust for some months.

Wearily, Edwina rose from her chair.

"Would you like it on a tray?" Vanessa asked.

"No, no, I'll be fine at the table," and Edwina shuffled into the kitchen, cautiously sitting down.

"This looks delicious," she said as they placed a small portion on her table mat.

They spent the next half hour chatting. Vanessa told her mother that Dan and Ross had enjoyed a boys' night out watching England play France in a football international at Wembley.

Edwina, in a clear voice, completely in tune, started singing the French anthem.

"Allons enfants de la patrie. Le jour de gloire est arrive."

Open mouthed, Vanessa and Diana waited for her to complete the entire rendition before breaking into laughter and applause.

"How do you know that?" Vanessa asked.

"Our French teacher at the Masonic school made us sing it at the start of every lesson—Madame Barneville. She was a bitch," Edwina said with feeling.

They all laughed and Vanessa felt a catch in her throat— it was like old times, shared laughter and family time.

"I can't believe you can sing the Marseillaise in perfect French from 1930 but you can't remember what you had for breakfast," Diana commented, still chuckling.

"What can I say?" Her mother exclaimed with a twinkle in her eye, "I'm just that talented."

Chapter 22

The three of them sat on the orange plastic chairs in the hospital out-patients. It was crowded and noisy with the hustle and bustle of nurses and doctors walking between rooms with determination. There was a wall mounted large screen TV playing rolling headlines from the BBC News Channel.

Edwina looked bewildered.

She'd received an appointment to see the urologist and Vanessa and Diana had collected her that morning from Sunset House for the short drive to the hospital.

The morning had been challenging as the 9:30 appointment meant they'd both had an early start, Vanessa picking Diana up en-route. They'd specifically asked for Edwina to be ready to leave but as both her girls were as efficient as their mother, they'd arrived at the home in plenty of time.

Just as well—Edwina was sat in her window chair, finishing her toast and marmalade, watching television.

Diana sighed.

"Morning, Mummy, how are you today?"

Edwina looked surprised to see them but gave a cheery greeting.

"Are you nearly ready to go?" Vanessa said, though clearly their mother was far from it. "Yes, I won't be a minute."

She pushed her laptop table back, spilling the remnants of her tea onto the table.

"Morning, lovelies, you're keen today."

A cheerful greeting from Brenda, one of the care assistants, as she went past Edwina's door.

"We've got the hospital appointment in a bit and need to get going."

Diana's retort managed to be both friendly and biting in equal measure. To be fair, both women were annoyed that their request for Edwina to be ready had been ignored.

"Oh my, let's get you going then." Brenda bustled into the room.

"Sorry, I didn't know. We're a bit short staffed today. Come along, my love, where's your shoes and coat?"

They were both very fond of Brenda—a practical no-nonsense woman who barely touched five feet in height, she was nonetheless a powerhouse of authority and organisation. Immensely kind, but not one to take any nonsense, both Diana and Vanessa felt sorry for their abruptness.

"It's ok, not your fault, it just takes a while to get her anywhere."

"My handbag, where's my handbag?"

Edwina had succumbed to having her coat put on and her slippers replaced with flat walking shoes.

"I've got it, Mummy."

"Give it to me." Edwina almost snatched it from her youngest daughter and began fiddling with the contents.

"My glasses, my keys?"

"They're all there," Diana reassured her.

Whilst she had no need for house keys, she was paranoid about going through her usual routine as if she was leaving her own home and they both agreed to capitulate and pretend it was normal but god, it was hard to keep your temper.

Taking Edwina through reception to the car park, she waved at the staff on the desk and thanked them for looking after her.

Diana looked heavenward and the two-reception staff laughed and told Edwina to have a nice day.

Once seated in the BMW, she chatted animatedly until they pulled up at the hospital entrance. Diana nipped out and took Edwina's arm, as Vanessa unclipped her seatbelt. Released from the safety catch, Edwina became confused again. Checking for her stick and handbag, she asked Diana how much she owed the driver.

"Don't worry, Mummy, I'm doing it for love," laughed Vanessa.

"She's just going to find a space in the car park and then she'll join us. Let's go and find a seat."

Diana steered Edwina towards the reception desk, appointment letter in hand.

Vanessa did a couple of circuits of the car park waiting for a space to appear. As always, with a weekday of out-patient appointments, the car park was packed, but Vanessa headed towards the furthest point from the entrance. Sure enough, there were spaces under the trees, but obviously being an extra few paces from the main front door, these were unpopular with the vast majority of visitors. To be fair, Vanessa mused as she reversed into an available space, without Diana here, Edwina would not have been able to walk that far to the hospital doorway.

So, now they sat, waiting for Edwina to be called. They'd tried chatting to her but she was evidently struggling with both the noise of the waiting area and the confusion in general about why she was there, so they resorted to talking to each other about mundane daily things in order to pass the time.

A young nurse shouted, 'EDWINA THOMPSON' and both Diana and Vanessa stood up. Diana smiled at the nurse, as her sister helped Edwina to stand.

"Where are we going?"

"To see Mr Edwards, the doctor."

Somewhat unsteadily, they walked her down the corridor. The nurse had set off at a pace, but realising Edwina was never going to keep up, she smiled apologetically and slowed her speed, stopping at an open doorway and gesturing them in with her hand.

A burly man sat at the desk by the window. Dressed in chinos and an open necked checked shirt, he looked at Edwina and immediately stood up, all six feet plus of him coming towards her with an outstretched hand, the size of a bear paw. For a man of his size, he had a surprisingly quiet voice, exuding calm with a Welsh lilt.

"Well, good morning, Mrs Thompson, a pleasure to meet you. See you've got the whole team here today."

He smiled at Vanessa and Diana and there was a twinkle in his blue eyes.

He's good, thought Diana. Something about the fact he'd taken in their mother's demeanour in seconds and his old-fashioned greeting to her, immediately warmed the trio to the man in front of them.

"Good morning, doctor," Edwina beamed in her best telephone voice.

"Let's get you a seat." He gestured towards a plastic chair by the window, but immediately replaced it with his own padded chair.

The replacement had arms and he helped Edwina lower herself into it.

"Now then, you sit yourself on this one," he indicated the plastic chair to Vanessa, whilst he grabbed a wheeled stool and perching somewhat precariously on it, propelled himself to his desk.

"And you, m'dear," he looked at Diana, "can rest yourself on the bed."

He indicated the examination bed, jutting out into the room. He laughed.

"I think you might have the comfiest seat in the house!"

Diana laughed and sat down.

"Now then, Mrs Thompson, how are you doing? I'm sorry we never got to meet whilst you were staying here but it's good for us to have a catch up. Tell me a bit about yourself."

"I'm very well, thank you. I live alone, my husband died some years ago."

"What did he do?"

"He was a merchant seaman."

"Really, a travelling man. I bet he saw some great places."

Edwina had visibly relaxed.

"Oh yes, we had some wonderful trips together."

"How did you meet?"

Mr Edwards was fully concentrating on Edwina—no note taking, or hurrying her through, just a relaxed chat.

"We met at church. I was 12 and he was 13. He was in the choir." Edwina gave a small smile.

"So, childhood sweethearts! What did you do for a living?"

"I was in the Wrens in the War—James was at sea then and I worked in the War Office."

"Goodness, a responsibility at that young age. Did you enjoy it?"

"I LOVED it," Edwina replied and Vanessa, who knew her mother's history of employment, was surprised by the passion and delight Edwina showed in recollecting her past. She'd never appreciated how much the job had meant to the young woman and for the first time, she became aware that her mother had experienced an exciting young adulthood and had a history that her daughters had unintentionally dismissed.

"So," Mr Edwards was gently steering Edwina back to the present day. "You live alone. How do you manage?"

"Very well, I live in a bungalow, lots of lovely neighbours and friends and I keep busy in my garden."

Diana realised that either intentionally or accidentally, Edwina was giving a somewhat sugar-coated view of her circumstances.

"Mummy's been in a nursing home though since she was discharged. She needed some help looking after herself."

"Oh yes, but I've gone back home now. I have my husband to look after," her mother interjected.

Mr Edwards nodded, then looked at Vanessa, sitting alongside her mother. She gave a slight shake of her head and he, almost imperceptibly, nodded.

"Now then, you do know that we found this tumour in your bladder when you were here with us?"

Edwina nodded. "I don't know how I picked it up."

He smiled. "Well, these things are a bit of a bugger. Is there any family history of cancer?"

"No," she replied.

Diana interjected again.

"Our grandmother died of breast cancer."

"Maternal." Vanessa added.

"No, she didn't," Edwina said heatedly. "I'm seeing her for lunch later," and she tutted at them both.

Mr Edwards kept writing, but Vanessa saw a ghost of a smile cross his face.

"Well, we have some options I'd like to go through with you."

He put his pen down and leaned forward looking directly at Edwina.

"Firstly, you understand that this is a cancer?"

Edwina nodded.

"Now, we can put you on the operating list to have it removed, but that comes with its own problems."

"Yes, I understand I might not survive."

"Dying isn't the problem, m'dear. You may well survive, but given your age, and…" he glanced back at her medical history, "given you've had a couple of minor strokes in the past, there's a very real chance you could have a massive stroke during the operation. Now, that might well kill you, or it might leave you in a paralysed or vegetative state. Either way, it wouldn't be an outcome that would improve your quality of life. Frankly, dying on the table might be the better option."

Blimey, thought Diana, *he didn't mince his words!*

He continued, all the while maintaining his gaze on Edwina.

"The alternative is we take a more pragmatic approach. I would guess this has been brewing for some time, so it's only started impacting on you fairly recently. Our other option is to leave well alone and let nature take its course. I think at your age, that might also be the kindest option."

Mr Edwards stopped talking, giving them all a chance to digest the information.

Edwina was nodding but no one was convinced she entirely understood the implications of what he was saying. Vanessa decided to grasp the nettle. Holding her mother's hand, she looked him in the eyes.

"So, you're saying do nothing and wait for it to kill her?"

"In effect, yes. We would obviously keep you comfortable." Again, he focused entirely on Edwina.

"And I'd like to see you every couple of months, but given your age and history, I think this is the wisest and kindest route."

"Mummy does have a Living Will," Diana said.

He nodded. "Then this plan would fit in with those wishes."

"Can you tell us a bit more about the..." Vanessa struggled to find the right word.

"The progress of the disease?" Mr Edwards put in helpfully.

"Yes."

"The tumour will grow, we don't know how fast and without an operation to grade it, I don't know how aggressive it is. But given the symptoms of the bleeding when she was admitted, I would estimate that it could take anywhere between three and twelve months. As the tumour grows, it begins to block the tubes and passages and there's always the chance it will spread to other organs. There's a build-up of toxins affecting the kidneys, which can then often cause confusion. There's extreme tiredness and then unconsciousness before you gently fade away. Honestly, it's probably one of the better ways to go."

He gave a gentle smile to Edwina.

"You don't have to make any decisions today. I just want to give you all the information and then you and your team," he gestured to Vanessa and Diana, "can have a talk through and decide."

"I don't want surgery. I'm an old lady. I've had a good life, been very lucky. Whatever happens, happens."

Mr Edwards nodded and leant in towards her.

"You can always change your mind. I'd rather not put you through an operation, but if it's what you want, we will do so."

Diana wanted some concrete information.

"Mummy's in the nursing home at the moment but would like to go home. What do you recommend?"

"She's going to get weaker and probably quite confused. I don't mean next week, but over time, it will start impacting on other systems. How confused is she?"

"She struggles sometimes with knowing who we are. Not all the time but since she was admitted here, it's been more noticeable, but we don't know if that's the illness or if she's become a bit institutionalised. She was always pretty sharp."

He smiled at Edwina, keeping hold of her hand.

"I can imagine no one got much past you."

She chuckled and lowered her eyes.

Oh god, she's gone all flirty, thought Vanessa.

"I'd honestly say, it's likely to be the disease. It's hard without the histology, but I think it's clear the cancer has been in situ for some time and so, it's highly likely to be related. I'd be uncomfortable if she was living alone."

"She gets very agitated about weeing. Would it be possible for her to have the catheter again?" Vanessa asked.

"I'd not recommend it at present. We know she's pulled it out before and every time she's likely to do some damage. Frankly, with the tumour, it's probably pretty aggravating."

"Not a suprapubic one?" Vanessa ventured.

He looked up at her.

"Nurse?"

"Urology sec."

He smiled again and nodded.

"Miss it?"

"Absolutely."

"We're the best of the bunch! But I'd not advise a suprapubic one. More chance of infections and she's still likely to pull at it. Maybe later on."

"Now, I'm going to put a note on the system. It's likely that as things progress, you may go into retention. In which case, they'll bring you into A&E and some gung-ho registrar will start poking around and inserting things to unblock you. That's going to be uncomfortable and prolong things, doing you no favours."

He was busy typing as he spoke.

"If you get brought in, make sure they call one of my team and we'll come and sort things. Now, m'dear, any questions?"

Edwina, who had been struggling to follow all the conversation—she was very tired—started putting on her gloves.

"No, thank you, doctor. Thank you for everything."

"You're most welcome. We'll get another appointment arranged for eight weeks and I'll meet up with you and 'your sisters' again then. In the meantime, if you have any questions, ring my secretary. Now, ladies, I think you all need to go out and have a coffee and a cake."

Laughing, Edwina stood up, leaning heavily on her stick. She shook Mr Edwards' hand and leaning on Vanessa's arm headed towards the door. He shook hands with Diana and Vanessa, saying in a hushed tone. "Call if you need anything. It's the best decision."

Thanking him and the nurse who had miraculously appeared in the doorway, they headed down the corridor.

"Would you like a coffee and cake on the seafront, Mummy?"

"No, thank you, dear. I'd like to go back now."

Vanessa went to the pay machine, slipped the car park ticket into the slot and paid the outstanding amount from the change in her purse. She then made her way back to the car park whilst Diana walked Edwina slowly towards the exit door.

"He was lovely, wasn't he?" Diana said to her mother.

"Yes, dear, very. Looks like I'm a goner though!"

They drove back to Sunset House in silence, each woman lost in her own thoughts. Pulling up at the entrance, Diana came round to help Edwina from the front seat. She looked exhausted and the trip had obviously taken its toll physically as well as mentally. They were buzzed in by Elaine on reception who smiled warmly at them and asked if Edwina would like a cup of tea.

"That'd be lovely, dear, thank you," and she slowly made her way round the winding corridors towards her room.

And there, sitting in the wing backed window chair sat a visitor.

"Jenny! Oh, my Jenny!" Edwina beamed as both Diana and Vanessa looked aghast at each other.

It seemed their ex-convict eldest sister was most definitely back on the scene!

Chapter 23

Jennifer Wozny, nee Thompson, had had an idyllic childhood. The only child for nine years, beloved by parents and grandparents, aunts and uncles, she had been spoilt with boundless love.

It wasn't unusual for her mother to receive a telegram from Jennifer's father telling them to meet him at some exotic port for a trip. Taken out of her all-girls' school, she and Edwina would fly or get the overnight train to Rotterdam, Naples, Athens or the West African coast, meet up with whatever ship James was commanding and spend days, sometimes weeks, in the cocoon of joyous family time together. All the sailors on board treated their captain's daughter with kindness and fun. Deck games of quoits in the warmth of an Italian evening, swimming trips off the coast of Capri or sailing north to Bergen, marvelling at fjords and the little islands they sailed past, were the rhythms by which Jennifer lived her early life. Born in the early 1950s, she was fortunate her school felt travel broadened the mind and her knack for picking up languages and absorbing geographical facts and historical information ensured she was a well-rounded young lady with the world at her feet.

When her sister Diana arrived on the scene, initially Jennifer was delighted—a real live baby doll to play with, but she soon realised that she was no longer the centre of attention and those long holiday excursions were becoming a thing of the past.

By the time Vanessa was born, Jennifer was in her mid-teens. Both her parents were in their forties—Vanessa being something of an unplanned addition—and Jennifer found the whole idea of her parents still having a productive sex life as something abhorrent and embarrassing.

Edwina had a difficult pregnancy and birth with Vanessa and whilst James had recently come ashore, he was still expected to travel the globe for the shipping company. Jennifer took on the role of surrogate mother to Vanessa for the first few months whilst her mother regained her strength but she did so with little good grace.

Jennifer knew from an early age that she could charm her way out of most situations. Her mother's deep brown eyes combined with naturally curly russet locks, meant that whilst she wasn't a classic beauty, she had an aura of confidence, sass and knew a wiggle of her hips could entice boys and men alike to do her bidding.

Jennifer was also a consummate liar.

She could look you direct in the eye and convince you it was a sunny mild day even when you knew torrential rain and biting winds were beating on the frosty window!

Jennifer was also a thief.

If she saw something she wanted, she took it. Starting with sweets from the newsagents when she was little, she progressed to make-up, records, cigarettes and alcohol as she got older. She thought nothing of taking cash from her mother's purse and as she got older, perfected the art of forging signatures, managing to access her sisters' post office savings accounts and later using their credit cards and writing cheques in their names. She acquired everything from shoes to plane tickets.

The combination of charm and lies was lethal—and Diana and Vanessa hated her.

When she was just 17, she'd been to an unauthorised party with some of her college friends and been found rolling around on the bed, devoid of her bra and knickers, with the son of the homeowners and his friend.

James, who loved her dearly, read her the riot act, shouting loudly and called her a slut. Privately, he had put his head in his hands, telling his wife 'she's like a dog on heat.'

Jennifer married before she was twenty—an older man, Phil, who neither of her parents liked or trusted. She had six children in quick succession and turned up one night on the Thompson's doorstep, having not seen or spoken to them in over three years. She was in debt, the bailiffs were coming to take away her furniture and her home and Phil had kicked her out.

James and Edwina bailed her out then and multiple times in the following years. Vanessa was only four when Jennifer married, so didn't really remember much about her sister being around. Diana had much clearer memories of Jen living at home but she was also aware of the nights she could hear her parents talking, worrying about trying to scrape funds together to avoid yet more of Jen's cheques bouncing. Diana was scarred by hearing her father crying when the mortgage company refused his guarantor's cheque. They'd fallen for that one too often with his daughter and therefore didn't trust the father either! James struggled with the fact that they'd question his word. A man of his generation, his honour and trust were the standard by which he set his life and to have it called into question destroyed his dignity and values.

A relatively normal period of time when Jennifer found work in a solicitor's office came to an abrupt end when she was charged with theft from her employer and spent two years in prison. It was the final straw for James, who never saw or spoke to her again.

After her father's death, Jennifer disappeared again, surfacing in Poland. Having married a young man Jakob, the same age as her eldest son and not having bothered with the legal niceties of getting divorced from Phil—they'd been separated for a dozen years—she added bigamy to her list of accomplishments. On her return to the UK, Vanessa and Diana had discovered Edwina had not only paid off Polish debtors, enabling her to leave the country, but had also invested in her new business of cake decorating. Tired of their mother's excuses about how tough Jennifer's life was, they'd both told Edwina they wanted nothing more to do with her.

The final straw for Edwina came four years earlier when Jennifer was charged and found guilty of fraudulent accounting and embezzlement of funds from the charity where she'd been working as an office manager. Over £300,000 had gone on holidays, new cars, new kitchen and new wardrobe. The charity had collapsed and the news hit the tabloids.

Vanessa and Dan had attended court to hear the verdict and the judge sentencing Jennifer to five years had commented that if she had put her undoubted talents into developing her own legitimate business, she would have been exceptionally successful.

Edwina told Vanessa and Diana that Jennifer was dead to her. She'd tried to pay some money to the charity to stop it from going bust, but the extent of Jennifer's theft was beyond even Edwina's means to recompense them.

And now, she was back.

Enveloping her mother in a hug, like she'd never been away.

Chapter 24

"Dizzy, Nessa." Jennifer acknowledged her younger sisters with their childhood names. They stared at her.

"Oh, my darling girl," Edwina said, shrugging off her coat and laying on her bed with her handbag.

"It's been so long. They," she looked pointedly at her other two daughters, "said you were dead!"

Jennifer arched a perfectly plucked eyebrow.

"Really?"

"No, Mummy, you said she was dead to you when she was sent to prison!" Diana's retort held the same stern tone as her mother's had.

Vanessa was in admiration for her elder sister. She'd never have been brave enough to say it as it was. Always rather nervous and in awe of Jennifer, she knew that she'd have bottled any confrontation. But Diana, self-assured in her knowledge of what was right, happily stood her ground, glaring right back at Jennifer.

Ignoring Diana's statement, Edwina turned to Jennifer.

"You'll stay for lunch? The hotel has a lovely dining room. I'll book us a table."

She half rose out of her chair, but Vanessa quickly interjected.

"I'll sort it, Mummy. We need to get back anyway so we'll leave you to it. I just need to pop to the loo."

She glanced at Diana and gathered up her coat, managing to pick up Edwina's bag in its billowing folds. She scooted down the corridor towards the visitors' toilet and once inside, she slid the bolt across. She removed her mother's house keys from the handbag and took £40 in ten-pound notes from Edwina's purse, leaving a five-pound note and some loose change.

Flushing the toilet so as not to arouse suspicion, she went back to her mother's room. Putting her mother's bag on the bed, Vanessa exclaimed, "What am I like, picked up the wrong bag! Now, Mummy, we'll be off, see you tomorrow with the boys."

She hoped referencing Jennifer's brothers-in-law, who detested her only marginally more than their wives, would deter Jennifer from visiting again tomorrow.

Grabbing Diana's arm, she blew a kiss to their mother and steered them back to the front door.

The got into Vanessa's BMW and she pulled out of Sunset House driveway onto the tree lined suburban street. Driving a couple of hundred yards down the road, she pulled in and turned the engine off.

"Fuck! Fuckity, Fuckity, Fuck Fuck!"

Not eloquent, not ladylike but it perfectly summed up Vanessa's feelings.

Diana was shaking. She'd lost all colour from her face and she stared at Vanessa. "Now what?"

"Now, we go to the house. We need to clear out the safe, jewellery, anything that she can get access to that will give her funds."

"Oh God, the keys," Diana exclaimed realising their mother's set of keys would provide easy access.

Somewhat triumphantly, Vanessa removed her mother's set of keys from her coat pocket. "I also took most of her cash from her purse, so there's only about ten pounds in total." Giving the cash to Diana, she said, "You keep hold of it with the financials. At least we've got the cheque books and bank cards and the Powers of Attorney and health documentation is all filed and in place, so we've done as much as we can. Call Michael and update him and ask him to tell Dan. We'll go to the house and secure what we can. I wonder how the hell she found out where Mummy was?"

They looked at each other and simultaneously said, "Edith!"

Vanessa started the car again and pulled out into the traffic whilst Diana dialled her husband on her mobile to regale him with the latest chapter in the saga.

Chapter 25

Vanessa's phone rang. She had spent the day trying to catch up with some work. It hadn't been easy to concentrate but it was also good to have something else to think about. The VAT return was due and whilst Dan had prepared it for submission, Vanessa was happy to be immersed in some sort of normality.

"Hello, darling," Edwina sounded chirpy.

Vanessa had a mix of delight and dread. It was a surprise that not only had her mother remembered her phone number, but she also seemed remarkably normal and with-it. Coupled with that feeling however was the pit in her stomach that her mother wanted something.

Feeling guilty and hopeful in equal measure, Vanessa saved her excel document, ready to give full attention to Edwina. With the phone nestled between her ear and shoulder, she typed and talked.

"Hello, how are you today?"

"Fine, darling. I'm sorry to trouble you but I wondered if you could give me a lift home?" *Bollocks,* thought Vanessa. She genuinely had a full day ahead of her. Not only had work been neglected but so had the house. There was no food in the fridge, Simba needed walking and she had to arrange her car service which was long overdue.

She'd been planning on driving down to Eastbourne the following day and take her mother for tea on the seafront at the Wish Tower. A favourite haunt of her parents, Vanessa had thought it would be nice to be out of the nursing home for a couple of hours. Diana and Michael were in America visiting Mark and Ruth. A delayed trip, they'd gone last week so the burden of visiting Edwina had fallen to Vanessa. No, she mustn't think of it as a burden or duty. It was just noticeable, with Diana away, how much they shared the load normally.

"I'm sorry, Mummy, I'm snowed under today."

It wasn't a lie and it wasn't like Vanessa was round the corner and could take a half hour out of her morning. It would be a whole day event and trying to wrestle her mother back to the nursing home took some patience and frankly a bit of sneakiness.

"I could come down tomorrow. Is it urgent?" She queried, though couldn't imagine what would warrant any urgency.

"Don't worry, love, I'm all packed up. I can get a taxi."

"What do you mean, you're all packed up? You do remember, you can't stay at home at the moment." Vanessa was now on high alert.

"Well, of course I would, it's my home! I've been here long enough and it's not cheap, you know." Edwina sounded indignant.

"The garden will need sorting and there's bills to pay."

Vanessa rubbed her eyes wearily.

"You know you can't stay on your own, Mummy. It's not safe. You need to have your tablets regularly and you don't want to end up back in hospital."

Edwina made a 'pfft' sound down the phone.

"I'm perfectly fine. You can't stop me."

Technically, she was right. The nursing home had made it clear to them that if Edwina wanted to leave, they couldn't stop her walking out the front door.

However, the mere fact that both Diana and Vanessa knew she was increasingly forgetful was a worry. Suppose she left the hob on, or forgot to lock up? Suppose some shyster (Vanessa conjured up an image of Jennifer) came knocking and Edwina fell for their flannel?

She tried another tack.

"You know we've talked about this. Daddy would want you to be safe. He'd expect us to make sure you didn't come to any harm. He'd be seriously miffed if we didn't look after you."

"Oh, love," Vanessa could almost hear her mother smiling down the phone. "Hitler didn't get me with his bombs, did he? If I survived that, I'll be fine. And anyway, I'll speak with daddy when he's home for dinner and he'll understand."

"I think we can both agree that you'll be safe from Hitler bombing you tonight," her daughter replied somewhat sarcastically and then thoughtlessly, "and daddy won't be home for dinner, he's been dead 25 years!" Silence.

More gently she added, "You aren't well enough to look after yourself."

It was true that physically Edwina was in a much better place than a few months ago when she collapsed. There was little obvious signs as yet that the cancer was causing any bodily weakness, though her mind was increasingly confused and befuddled.

Once again, she rubbed her eyes.

"Look, how about I come down tomorrow and we can go to the bungalow for you to check it? Bob's been coming in, so the garden is tip top and we've bought you all the post, so Diana's been making sure the bills are paid."

"She has no bloody right," Edwina spat out.

"How dare she? Interfering in my affairs. The bitch. I'll have words when I see her." The change in tone and the vitriol in her mother's voice took Vanessa by surprise, though these outbursts were becoming more frequent.

Again, she didn't know what was the disease and what was pure frustration on Edwina's part. It was important not to react, though God knows what she says about me thought Vanessa.

"Now, come on, Mummy. You know you asked her to write the cheques for you and to make sure everything was paid on time. She's done a fantastic job of keeping everything going for you." More bravely, she added, "I'm disappointed in you speaking like that about Diana. I thought better of you." Silence.

Vanessa hoped it was sinking into Edwina's head that she was being unreasonable.

"Look, it's nearly lunchtime. You get something to eat and I'll be down first thing in the morning and we'll pop home and then maybe go out for lunch. How's that sound?"

"Fine," Edwina muttered somewhat begrudgingly in a tone of a sulky teenager.

The phone went dead.

Vanessa took a sip of her coffee that had been rapidly cooling on the side. Knowing the following day would be a trial, particularly convincing Edwina to return to the nursing home, she determined was to have a productive day and concentrate on her own requirements.

Having submitted the VAT return and responded to a dozen emails, she popped into town to buy some chicken for dinner, collected Dan's suit from the dry cleaners and stood in a long line at the post office to send a birthday gift to her best friend in Australia.

Dumping the chicken in the fridge on her return home, she wrestled an excited Simba into his harness, picked up poo bags and her phone, attached his extendable lead and got pulled out the door and up the road. Heading down the woodland walk at the back of their house and into the orchards beyond, for the first time in a days, Vanessa enjoyed some warm sunshine on her face. Simba busily snuffled amongst the grass, nipping off the odd dandelion—his favourite—as he exercised his brain as much as his body with the tantalising countryside smells. Vanessa was content to amble and stop at regular intervals to allow him to fully investigate every blade of grass.

The recent rains and warm sunshine had brought a carpet of bluebells out and in the quiet of the path, with only the crunching of wood-chippings under her feet, she began to feel revived and refreshed. Vanessa loved her dog walks, especially on her own. She naturally enjoyed the weekend hikes with Dan and the dog but they rarely just walked. Often the conversation was peppered with work, kids, money and because he was so much taller than Vanessa, his lolloping long gait meant a walk for him was invariably a gentle canter for her just to keep up with him. There was often the refrain of 'slow down, I've only got little legs.'

On her own, she could go at her own pace, and enjoy the scenery. Of course in the daily bustle, a quick run around the block a couple of times a day was often the usual exercise, but if she had time and frankly the inclination, she loved a dog walk on her own.

Vanessa was very good at finding excuses for not doing something. To be fair when juggling the balls of life, she always put herself at the back of the list. Dan would religiously go to the gym four times a week and if something needed doing, he'd crack on straight away. That didn't translate into household jobs like filling the washing machine or doing the shopping. For an enlightened soul, he had been known to mutter (in jest and with a wink) 'that was bird's work.' However, he was your man for any handy jobs around the house and should Vanessa ask him to hoover or do the dishwasher, he'd do a thorough job. It was also true that Vanessa was someone who thought that no one could do the job as well as she could and therefore often refused help to make sure the job was done properly. She blamed her mother. Edwina had had a cleaning lady for many years who came in twice a week and Edwina was famous for cleaning through before Mrs Baker arrived.

"I don't want her thinking the house is filthy," was her reasoning for this. It caused James to put his head in his heads and her daughters much hilarity, but secretly they knew where their mother was coming from and she'd passed the weird logic on to them.

So, whilst Vanessa pledged to do Pilates three times a week, or go swimming every morning at 6:30 and whilst in her mental diary, she'd change the beds and towels every Monday, in reality, she'd end up ironing instead of exercising and the housework could be on an ad hoc basis, usually when clouds of Simba's fur could be seen under the armchair.

Today, though felt like a good day. Returning from her walk, she prepared a chicken jambalya in the slow cooker, spent twenty minutes pulling up some weeds in the front garden and caught up with an episode of Grey's Anatomy whilst having a sandwich for her lunch.

She was about to head back into their garden office mid-afternoon to check on her emails when the phone rang.

"Hello, Barnes Construction."

"Vanessa? It's Cynthia from Sunset House. It's about Edwina."

"Is she ok?"

"We just wanted to let you know, she's gone home." "What! When? How?"

"About half an hour ago. She got a taxi. She's taken a bag with her but we thought you should know. Your sister was with her."

For a second, Vanessa was confused. Di was in New York. Then it registered—Jennifer. Shit!

"We thought you should know, your sister said that as she's the next of kin, we need to update our records. We obviously know there's been some issues in the past and you and Diana are Edwina's named kin for the Power of Attorney, so nothing has changed on her records here but we thought you should be aware."

Vanessa's mind was racing. What was Jennifer up to? More to the point, they still had the keys to the house, so how would Edwina get in? Would they lose her room at Sunset House?

"I'll sort it out, thanks so much for letting me know. Can you hold her room?"

"You've paid for the next month anyway, so that's not a problem for now. She can obviously come back whenever."

"Great, thank you. Speak soon."

Vanessa put the phone down with a trembling hand. Her hatred of everything Jennifer stood for made her seethe and she appreciated this was the reason for the reaction. Her eldest sister had stolen and lied to her family for as long as Vanessa could remember and now, her vulnerable and confused mother was at the mercy of her unscrupulous daughter.

Deciding not to tell Diana—she couldn't do anything anyway and why ruin her holiday—Vanessa picked up her mobile and sent a WhatsApp message to Dan on their Hubby/Wifey group.

"I need to go to Mummy's. Jennifer has taken her out of Sunset and gone with her to the bungalow. I need to sort out."

She almost instantly saw two ticks to say the message was delivered.

Dan typing…came up.

"On my way, wait for me. We'll go together."

Relieved at his response, Vanessa sat on the bottom stair and wept…Simba sat alongside her, head on her knee and for once, his pneumatic tail fell silent and still.

Chapter 26

They drove in virtual silence. Vanessa looked out of the window of the passenger seat but not really seeing anything going past.

As they pulled up on Edwina's driveway, she gave a huge sigh as if she'd been holding her breath for the last thirty miles. Dan looked at her, squeezed her hand and said, "Ready?" She nodded and got out of the car with none of the determination that she felt. Driving down she'd clarified in her own mind this mustn't be about the animosity she felt towards Jennifer. This was about the care and safety of Edwina. Keep focused on that…keep focused on that.

They went round to the back gate and getting her mother's house keys in her hand, she tried the door. It was unlocked. Vanessa had realised on the way down, the neighbours had a spare set, so that would have been how they'd got access.

There was a murmur of voices from the lounge and quietly shutting the back door, Dan and Vanessa walked through the kitchen and into the lounge.

Edwina looked up from her armchair in the corner of the room and beamed a welcome. Jennifer looked rather more surprised to see her youngest sister with her husband standing behind her.

Jennifer had always rather fancied Dan. He was obviously younger than her but he kept himself fit and she definitely would, given the chance!

"Darling, how lovely to see you! Daniel, what a surprise, come on in." Edwina looked tired but settled.

Crossing the room to kiss her mother, Vanessa's face softened. She bent down and touched the papery soft cheek to her own. Her mother smelt of a mixture of her favourite perfume—Lancome, La Vie Est Belle—and, well, frankly, urine! It just made Vanessa feel sad.

She turned her attention to Jennifer.

"I'll make another cuppa," Jennifer said, as if the arrangement was nothing out of the ordinary. "There's only powdered milk, I'm afraid. Nothing in the fridge."

Vanessa was tempted to say, of course not, you stupid cow, she's been in a nursing home for the last five months. Instead, she took a deep breath and steadied herself.

"No, thank you. But I'd be interested to know what you're playing at?"

Edwina eyed her daughters. She'd picked up on a change in the atmosphere but wasn't sure why.

"I'm not playing at anything. I visited her this morning and she wanted to come home, so I've brought her home. Something, I believe you refused to do!"

"And how, pray, did you get here?" There was no car on the drive and as far as Vanessa was aware, Jennifer had no means to purchase one.

"By taxi, of course," her sister replied somewhat sarcastically. "Come on, Ness, have a tea and chill."

Vanessa resisted the urge to slap Jennifer. "And how did you pay for the taxi? Mummy doesn't have much cash on her."

"It's on account." Edwina answered. "They always bring me up from Morrisons with the shopping, so they know I'm good for it."

Vanessa thought, *God, Jennifer's only been back for a few days and already she's running up bills for someone else to pick up!*

"Jennifer's going to move in with me. We're going to live together. Won't that be lovely? I'll have some company and Jennifer can take care of everything for me." Edwina beamed. Vanessa could have screamed.

She wanted to shout at her mother. "Don't you remember what she did? Don't you remember how she hurt you and daddy? Don't you remember how frightened you were about her turning up on the doorstep? How can you even think about having her under your roof?"

Instead, she patiently said to Edwina, holding her hand, "But you need nursing care, Mummy. That's why you're at Sunset House. Remember the doctor said as time goes on, you'll need more and more care by professionals. Visiting home is absolutely fine, we can do it every day if you want to, but you can't stay here."

"She can do whatever she wants. I'll make sure she's ok." Jennifer cocked her head on one side and looked at Vanessa with something of a smirk playing around her mouth. "I'm sorry," Vanessa whipped round to face her older sister. "I wasn't aware you'd qualified as a palliative care professional whilst you were inside!"

From his armchair in the corner of the room, Vanessa caught a hint of a smile on Dan's face.

"She's my mother!" Jennifer responded as if that was a suitable answer.

"She's OUR mother! And you've not been bothered over the last 25 years to worry about her. Where were you when she had a stroke, had her hips replaced and her shoulder op? Why now all of a sudden do you care? Nothing to do with your present post-prison circumstances I suppose?"

Vanessa's plan to keep this civil was rapidly going out the window. She'd forgotten the ease with which Jennifer could push emotional buttons.

"I'm the eldest and therefore her next of kin. This was my home too and you can now step back and let me take my turn in shouldering the burden!"

"Number 1—this was never your home. You buggered off long before we came here. Number 2—you may be the eldest but being next of kin is not a birth right. You earn that privilege and you've long since expired that option. Number 3—don't you EVER call Mummy a burden."

Jennifer went to answer, but Vanessa was on a roll.

"And how are you going to take care of her? Diana and I are jointly responsible for her finances and her health and you can be certain that we'll NEVER let you anywhere near her in trying to use her funds. You've broken her heart time and again, so you can think again if you're planning on moving in." Vanessa was breathing hard. Jennifer's eyes narrowed and she held the gaze of her sister.

"Di will agree with me—having mother home will be the best for everyone. It's where she wants to be and after all, we did spend nine years, just the two of us in the early days. We'll be fine and she can die happily in her own bed. You seem to forget, Nessa, you're the baby of the family. Leave it to the grownups to make the decisions."

"That's enough," Dan said quietly from his seat in the corner. "Don't you speak to my wife like that. You gave up your right to have any say in Edwina's welfare when you stole money and dragged the Thompson good name through the mud and the national press."

He looked at Edwina who was watching him. Dan had skilfully repeated an often-heard phrase of Edwina's about Jennifer's behaviour and he knew the distress she felt that James' family name had been splashed across the local and national papers in her fraud trial. He had calmly but cleverly reminded his mother-in-law of the recent past.

"The very mention of your name distressed her, so I'm surprised that you feel you have some God-given right to even be here, never mind dictating the future arrangements."

Jennifer looked at Dan. "Well, thanks for that, Bob the Builder, but I don't see it's any of your business."

"It became my business when your father, as he lay dying, asked Michael and me to make sure you never again hurt your mother."

"Enough!" Edwina said with more vigour than she had previously demonstrated.

"I'll not have bad behaviour in my house. Daniel is right, Jennifer. I'm heartsick at how you've behaved and I'm not stupid enough not to remember what you did to those poor charities. I'm disgusted by your lack of remorse. Your father would be so ashamed if he was here!"

Vanessa couldn't help but look somewhat triumphant at Jennifer. In a quieter voice, Edwina continued, "But I do want to come home. I know I need some help for a little while and I know you want what's best for me." She touched Vanessa's face as she knelt by her mother's feet. "But I just want to come home."

"And if I'm here, you can, from tonight!" said Jennifer.

"I know," Vanessa said, looking at Edwina as if Jennifer hadn't spoken. "Let's investigate what we can do about a live-in carer."

"I'm a live-in carer," Jennifer retorted somewhat acrimoniously.

"You're supposed to care for the other person, not yourself," Dan said quietly.

"Ha, ha, highly amusing...Not," replied his sister-in-law.

"The fact is, you have no experience of caring for a dying woman." Vanessa decided not to sugar coat the truth. "You have no access to funds to buy food, pay the bills or heat the house."

"Mother does though—I can do all that for her."

Vanessa looked blankly at her sister as if she'd not said anything.

"So, you responsibly bring her home, with no medication. You don't know what she takes or when she takes it. You don't know how to clean and treat her vaginal soreness because of the excoriation of her skin."

Dan shifted uncomfortably in his seat.

"You can't get her in the bath or shower as she can't climb into the bath and has no hoist." Jennifer cut her off with a wave of her hand. "All details we can sort easily enough. That's your trouble, Nessa, always so negative."

Vanessa could happily have slapped her.

Turning back to her mother she said, "You can't stay tonight. There's no food, the bed's not been aired, you've no tablets or pads here. I know you want to move back and I PROMISE you, we'll try and find a way to make it work so you can. We had to change the house insurance to an unoccupied property, so we need to amend that too. So, for now, staying here is just not feasible."

She stared at her mother, willing her to understand.

"Alright, dear, but can I stay for a bit longer today?"

Vanessa smiled. "Of course you can and then Dan and I can drop you back later when you're ready."

"I'll take you later," Jennifer said to her mother. "Whenever you want."

"No, you won't," Dan said quietly but in a tone that brooked no argument. Pulling out his phone, he said, "Would you like me to check the bus times for you?"

"What, no lift back for me?"

He smiled and shook his head.

"Well, I'll take myself off to the loo before I go. I presume that's allowed?"

"Be my guest," said Vanessa. "You sit there, Mummy, and we'll just wash up."

Edwina closed her eyes and Vanessa picked up the tray, carrying it into the kitchen. Jennifer walked the length of the hallway, turning left into the bathroom. The yellow suite was the original from 1972 with the sink inlaid in a Formica faux wooden vanity unit. Vanessa crept down the hall, waiting for her sister to emerge. She could hear Jennifer opening the vanity unit drawers and the cupboard behind the bath where her mother stored towels, toilet rolls, hot water bottles and umpteen gifts of bubble bath and talc from birthdays and Christmas' past.

As Jennifer exited the bathroom, she was greeted by Vanessa, Dan watching from the end of the hallway. Swinging in her hand, Vanessa held a keyring with two keys attached—one a short yale type lock and the other a long-shafted key. Edwina had always kept her safe keys hidden under the towels in the bathroom cabinet to fool any burglars, always assuming it would be the last place they looked.

"Looking for these?" She enquired of her sister.

For a fraction of a second, Jennifer looked both awkward and guilty.

"No, I was looking for a clean towel."

"You missed the one on the radiator then? The safe keys are no longer kept on the premises. Nor are any cheque books, bank cards, or share certificates. Everything of value is off-site."

"You really think I'd sink that low?" Jennifer said, eyeing the safe keys in her sister's hand.

"Legal requirement of the insurance—jewellery, paintings, keepsakes—anything worth anything is safely away from here. Just to be on the safe side you—know, in case anyone managed to break in. Can't be too careful nowadays. And yes, as you ask, I do think you'd sink that low. Remember the cheque book you stole from me and the credit cards you lifted from Diana's purse. The spending spree you went on using our bank accounts and credit cards running up hundreds of pounds of debt is burned into our memories! Which reminds me, can I have the keys?"

"What keys, I don't have any keys."

"Well, presumably you got in using the neighbours' set and I'll need to give them back."

"No, no, we used Mummy's keys—they were in her bag."

"No, they weren't," hissed Vanessa.

"Yes, they were."

From her other hand, Vanessa held up her mother's house keys.

"No, they weren't because I have them! So," holding out her hand, "please stop pissing around and give me the keys."

From her coat pocket, Jennifer extracted the duplicate set that resided at Sandra and Tony's house, for use in an emergency.

Thrusting them into Vanessa's outstretched palm Jennifer headed for the front door.

"Not saying goodbye?" Dan enquired.

"Tell her I'll be seeing her soon," and with that Jennifer slammed the front door behind her, causing the vase of artificial flowers placed on the chest by the front door, to sway and the windows to rattle.

Vanessa let out a long breath. Dan put an arm round her shoulder, dropping a kiss onto the top of her head.

"You know she'll be back, right?" He said.

"I know. But at least for now, she knows there's nothing here worth nicking or selling. Can you rinse the cups out and I'll tell the neighbours not to give her the keys again? Then we can look at getting Mummy back to Sunset."

Chapter 27

Edwina sat in her window seat chair gazing out at the entrance door to Sunset House. In the last few weeks since her last trip home, she had resigned herself to the fact she wasn't going to die at home.

The girls, true to their word, had investigated having live-in carers at the bungalow but Edwina had put objections and obstacles in place for every suggestion they made. They all knew, though no one voiced it, that as soon as she could, Edwina would dismiss them to get her own way. The fact was she didn't want strangers living in her house. She didn't want someone organising her day and what she could and couldn't do. The irony that was exactly the situation she found herself in at the nursing home, wasn't lost on her! But at least here it wasn't her own home, with strangers poking about in her cupboards.

She wanted the freedom to shop when she wanted; to go out and weed the garden; to sit and watch Countdown.

She now accepted that she was both too exhausted to care and too tired to bother. Since the visit home with Jennifer, when it had all kicked off, she hadn't gone back. Despite Vanessa and Diana offering almost daily to take her, she just couldn't be bothered to make the effort and always made an excuse.

The pain and discomfort from the tumour was becoming her focus of every minute of every day. The dragging feeling and constant irritation was like a nagging toothache—always there, always affecting everything she did—there was no escape from it.

Her plan to fall quietly asleep in her armchair and slip away, surrounded by her photos and knick-knacks with the view of her beloved garden framed by the large picture window in the lounge, had been foiled. Now, she was left in limbo, waiting for the end and wishing the Grim Reaper would get on with it.

She saw Diana and Vanessa push the entry button at the front door. They saw her sitting in her chair and waved enthusiastically, but she ignored them—waving back was too much effort.

Chapter 28

"This is a lovely room," Diana said as they arrived in the large, bright, airy upstairs room at the back of Sunset House.

"And look, Mummy, you've got an en-suite toilet and sink. That's much nicer isn't it?" Edwina looked listlessly around the room, resting on her walking stick. It was much larger than her one downstairs, so it would be more expensive—and it was quieter, though the pervading smell of cottage pie dinners still lingered in the air.

"Mmm," she said unenthusiastically, fingering the counterpane on the bed.

"Do you think you'd prefer this room?" Vanessa pressed.

The increasing need for Edwina to use a commode and the subsequent constant aroma of urine that seeped into every corner of her room, her clothing and seemed to hang onto every fibre of her, had compelled her daughters to ask if there were any rooms with baths or showers available. This one had a toilet and sink which would afford some dignity for Edwina and hopefully help with the problems around hygiene. They were both distressed that their proud, fastidious mother had been brought so low by something beyond her control.

Vanessa had been somewhat disconcerted since arriving on the upper floor. Because the lift was relatively small—and because Diana had an absolute terror of lifts—she'd volunteered to take the stairs and meet Vanessa and Edwina at the top. Having manoeuvred their mother and her stick into the lift, Vanessa set about making small talk which was abruptly ended when Edwina looked at her and said, "I'm sorry, who are you?"

"I'm Nessa, Mummy. We're going to have a look at the new room for you."

Edwina had nodded and as the ancient lift jolted to a halt, she winced and then gingerly stepped out onto the landing. Diana noted her sister's face, but didn't know the cause of her confusion and sadness that was so clearly written across the younger woman's brow. "I'm happy where I am," Edwina now declared and made her way to the door.

She was dying. Whether that was in a room with a toilet or not wasn't really important. As they exited the lift on the ground floor, an enthusiastic young man asked if she'd like to join in the bingo in the lounge. Over his shoulder, Vanessa could see the room lined with armchairs around the outer walls and an assortment of elderly folk. Some were slumped awkwardly, some shuffling their slippers on the patterned carpeted. Others stared into the distance, not engaging with the 'Activities' leader who was trying to stimulate them with throwing soft balls and beanbags. Her high, overly enthusiastic voice reached Vanessa.

"Oh, well done, Barry, great throwing!"

Jesus, thought Vanessa, *it's like they're ancient children at a sports day.* She could have cried. *Dear God, I hope I never end up with people thinking I need a rendition of 'My Old Man's a Dustman' in order to make my day complete.* She admired the persistence of the staff in trying to liven up the day-to-day routine, but goodness it was depressing! "No, thank you, that's kind, but not right now," Edwina said to the bingo man, and slowly headed back to her room.

She sat in her window seat chair and turning to her daughters said, "I think I'll sleep for a while. See you soon," and with that she closed her eyes.

The two of them knew when they'd been dismissed and saying their goodbyes left Edwina contemplating a plate of grey looking cottage pie and ice cream that was being delivered as they exited the doorway.

Chapter 29

The warmth of the early summer sun fell on Edwina's face. The seagulls whirled above her head and the sound of the waves crashing far below was music to her ears.

Vanessa had decided that as the day was fine, she was taking her mother out. In truth, they'd gone less than a mile from Sunset House but with the help of a borrowed wheelchair they were now sat at the St Bede's end of Eastbourne seafront. The grass expanse behind them was littered with dog walkers and people sitting enjoying the summer sun. If they'd both been fitter they could have walked down the pathway towards the sea and spied Beachy Head lighthouse nestling at the foot of the cliffs.

Edwina tilted her face to the sun and smiled. She and James had lived not far from here after they were married and she had many happy memories walking and talking along this seafront. Jennifer had been born at the local maternity unit and taken her first chubby steps on the beach here. James used to drive along the seafront every summer in his later years, in their blue Humber Sceptre, taking in the lights strewn along the seafront as part of the summer season. Blackpool it wasn't but the decorated flower beds and sparkly lights linking the lampposts from the pier to the Wish Tower were always a marvel and it had become a tradition to do this on a Saturday evening and then stop for a Mr Whippy Ice-cream on the pebble beach. Of course, there were less cars around then but the girls still remembered it as part of their youth and James had delighted in driving as slowly as possible to see how many cars had backed up behind him.

Vanessa snapped open a Tupperware from the wicker basket she'd brought. Nestled inside were tomato sandwiches—on white bread, no crusts, and a sprinkling of salt, cut into dainty triangles, she offered one to her mother.

Edwina almost squealed in delight.

She had often told the story that on arriving at their hotel the night of their wedding, she and James were starving, having missed the opportunity to eat anything substantial at their wedding buffet. The only thing the hotel could muster was tomato sandwiches which, according to Edwina, were the best thing they'd ever tasted and their first proper meal together as a married couple.

She now dipped into the proffered box, taking a small triangle.

Vanessa knew her mother's appetite was diminishing but she'd taken the chance that she might just be able to tempt her with something small.

"There's some strawberries for after if you fancy them," she said, taking a small flask from the basket and pouring her mother a tea into a tiny China cup she'd bought with her. Edwina always favoured a cup over a mug and Vanessa thought these little things were what made her mother happy.

They'd both had hysterics in trying to get Edwina into the wheelchair on arrival. Having lugged it out of the boot and attempted to work out how it unfolded, Vanessa, had been as gentle as possible getting her mother out of the car and into the chair. Edwina's comment that it was just like getting on and off the commode had forced a quizzical look from her daughter and they'd both dissolved into fits of laughter.

For a while, they sat in companionable silence, looking out at the horizon and the small boats that were dotted on the water.

"Do you remember the line of traffic that built up behind Daddy's hearse?" Edwina suddenly said.

"He'd have been so delighted to hold everyone up."

Vanessa chuckled. Her father's cortege, coffin draped in Naval flag, had taken a detour to the crematorium, going right the way along the seafront. It was a thoughtful gesture of the funeral directors and in a day of overwhelming sadness, had made them all smile as the cars backed up behind them.

So, today was a day that Edwina remembered she was a widow—something that was happening less often, with her often fretting where James was and why he hadn't visited her.

"Have you thought about your funeral?"

"Nope."

"I wondered if you had a preference, for hymns or music, or whatever."

"Nope. I don't want anyone standing up and making speeches."

Edwina gazed out to sea.

"Would you like to see a vicar?"

Their mother had always professed a strong faith and given her practical nature, both Diana and Vanessa were a little surprised she'd not mentioned anything about her funeral once her diagnosis was confirmed. It was almost as if Edwina refused to accept her prognosis.

"Nope. I don't want a woman vicar to conduct the service," she'd added as an afterthought.

"Okaaay—anything else?"

"Nope."

She paused.

"Jennifer's not to come."

The finality of her statement meant that there was nothing more to be said and after a little while longer, they packed up their picnic and began the journey back to Sunset House.

Chapter 30

Dan came out into the garden with a glass of red and a gin and tonic. The family were sat around the table, strewn with crisps and nibbles and the BBQ sat expectantly in the corner, waiting to be fired up.

Caitlin and Sam were fiddling with their phones and Charlotte had her face turned up to the sky, feet resting on the wicker stool that was usually stored under the chairs. Ross lay the length of the garden swing seat, sunglasses shielding his eyes and a hand on the top of Simba's head. The Labrador was content. Everyone was home, there were steaks and sausages in sight and all was right with his world.

Dan passed the G and T to Vanessa who smiled her thanks.

They'd been having a catch up with all the news and it was a chance to think about something other than Edwina and her declining health. They hadn't said, but all the young adults thought Vanessa was looking drained.

She relished having her children home and whilst they were all absorbed in their own thing, she enjoyed having them back, even if it was just for the day. She stood up and took a wander down the garden, drink in hand. She had never enjoyed gardening. Edwina had always wanted the outside space to be neat and tidy so it had been a chore rather than a delight. But Vanessa realised as she was getting older, she really quite enjoyed it. She was even brave enough to share her digging space with the odd worm, though she still had a repulsion for slimy slugs. Dan said they were snails with no mortgage—"No house, geddit?" He said on more than one occasion, laughing at his own joke.

Dan and Ross were chatting about Ross' new car as Vanessa deadheaded a few violas and geraniums. The mini heatwave they were experiencing meant the contents of the pots were showing their colours to full effect and the gentle buzzing of the bees and the perfume from the lavender bushes was a balm to the soul.

The phone rang in the house.

Caitlin jumped up. "I'll get it," she said, as Simba abandoned Ross' attention and trotted in behind her in the hope that she was going into the kitchen for snacks.

She came out with the phone clamped to her ear, Simba following dejectedly behind her. "Yeah, all good. I'll pass you over to Mum," and handing the phone across mouthed "Auntie Di."

"Hi."

"Sorry to disturb the BBQ. Mummy's had a fall at Sunset and they are waiting for an ambulance."

"Bloody hell, do they know what she's done?"

Dan looked up, watching his wife.

"They think she might have broken her shoulder. But they're not sure if she's hit her head. They found her behind the bedroom door. I'm going to meet them at A&E."

"Ok, I'll be there shortly."

"No, no, don't worry. You've got the kids. I'll keep you posted."

"It's ok, I'll come. Dan can sort out the BBQ, I'll see you in a bit."

Explaining the situation, she apologised to the children and went inside to get her things. "You've been drinking," Dan said, sounding more than a little pissed off. He had thought they could have at least one day without his mother-in-law impacting on their plans. "I've had a sip—pop it in the fridge and I'll have it later."

Picking up her bag and her phone, she went and kissed them all goodbye. The girls gave her a hug and they all sent their love to their grandmother.

Dan walked out to the drive with her.

"Do the BBQ. Let's keep it as normal as possible. You deserve a break."

"So do you," he said with feeling. Recognising this wasn't the time for a battle he opened the car door.

"Let me know how you get on. Message me when you arrive."

"Will do."

She gave him a hug and briefly kissed him before settling herself into the car and heading off once again to the A&E department.

On arrival, it was heaving. Saturday afternoon sports injuries, sunburn and a chappy with a tea towel wrapped round his hand. His black apron with the statement 'Bear Grills,' indicated it may well be a culinary BBQ accident.

Diana was sitting on a plastic chair, fanning herself with a leaflet. The hospital either hadn't invested in, or hadn't turned on the air conditioning and it was stifling.

"Hi, any news?"

"They're checking her now. Doesn't look like anything is broken but they found her collapsed behind the door, so they want to check for head injuries. She's very confused apparently."

The week before the hospital consultant had changed Edwina's medication as she seemed to be in a constant cycle of urinary infections and this had added to her general confusion. He'd been quite up front and said it was difficult to tell whether it was the infections or she was suffering with brain secondaries to the primary tumour.

Vanessa was about to message Dan when a nurse came up to them.

"You can come through now. The doctor will be in to see her soon."

Chapter 31

Edwina looked pale and shaky. Her eyes were closed. She had a monitor on her finger and lay awkwardly on the bed, half sitting, half lying. Her blue floral summer dress, which was now several sizes too big for her was slightly askew as was her favourite beige cardigan, hole in one elbow, that was slung around her shoulders. Her trademark 'American Tan' stockings were encased in her faux velvet red slippers. Her string of favourite pearls (also fake), were in place around her increasingly gaunt neck. Her fine white hair was sticking up at different angles and clutched in her bony fingers was her trusty handbag.

Their proud mother, who always endeavoured to be bandbox smart and well put together resembled a bag lady who'd been found in a shop doorway. Whilst Vanessa appreciated the home had tried to make sure she had everything she needed before leaving in the ambulance, Edwina looked like she'd fallen in the dressing up box.

Neither of her daughters knew her favourite cardigan needed darning or they would have sorted it for her. Once again, the overpowering feeling that they were letting Edwina down, enveloped Vanessa. Taking a breath, she gently touched Edwina's hand, so she wouldn't be surprised when she opened her eyes.

Edwina didn't react and had obviously drifted off to sleep. Pulling up a plastic chair each, they settled themselves for yet another wait.

One of the delights both Diana and Vanessa enjoyed—which they knew was not always the case with siblings—was the ability to natter about anything and everything. In the old days when both were working full time, bringing up their families and living at opposite ends of the country, they'd always continued conversations as if one had only momentarily left the room. Their sense of humour was so similar they'd often just look at one another and fall into uncontrollable fits of laughter, to the amusement or consternation of others around them who weren't in on the joke. This easy-going companionship had seen them through tough times and both were grateful for the solidity of their friendship. Whilst Vanessa was often seen as the more sentimental of the two, Diana had a fierce protective loyalty to her little sister and would often send a small gift or card she'd seen somewhere that she knew Vanessa would appreciate and cherish.

So now, they quietly chatted together—everything from their gardens, their children, Masterchef and Downton Abbey, friends and holidays. Every few minutes, their eyes strayed to Edwina, who hadn't moved, but they kept their sentinel watch, ready to be there for her when she woke.

The heat in the department was draining. A few desolate fans were dotted around the cubicles, humming in an effort to cool the air around them, but mainly succeeded in just moving hot air around. Water jugs were filled with ice chips, soon dissolving on table tops, leaving warm puddles at their base. Vanessa and Diana fanned themselves with whatever was to hand and occasionally checked Edwina's forehead, placing damp paper towels on her face to keep her comfortable.

The curtain opened and a doctor entered accompanied by a young nurse. The doctor was a woman who was small in stature, wearing a stethoscope slung casually round her neck like a piece of artistic jewellery. She nodded perfunctorily at the sisters and then tapped Edwina briskly on the hand. Bending closely towards her face, she said in a voice that seemed too loud for her size, "MRS THOMPSON."

With a start, Edwina opened her eyes, immediately taking on the bewildered and confused look her daughters were becoming used to.

"Wakey wakey now. How are you feeling?"

Whilst speaking, she was reading from the chart that had resided at the end of the bed. "I'm very tired," Edwina replied, her voice shaky and thready and lacking the usual deference she applied when speaking to a doctor.

Briefly, the doctor made eye contact with her and then returned her gaze to the notes.

"You fell, yes? Did you black out?"

"I don't know."

"What year is it?"

"Pardon."

"Can you tell me what year it is?"

This random question seemed to throw Edwina. The view of her daughters was blocked by the doctor but she knew this was a test she would need to pass. "17."

"Good."

She was about to write something in the notes when Edwina's next comment stopped her. "1917. Is the War over yet?"

Diana bit her lip and was about to say something when Vanessa stood up, and moving past the doctor took Edwina's hand, smiling gently. Edwina visibly relaxed.

"I understand our mother fell this afternoon and injured her shoulder? She's under Mr Edwards in urology for terminal bladder cancer."

Said firmly but perfectly pleasantly, Vanessa looked enquiringly at the doctor.

"Your mother has dementia," she stated. "We'll get a CT scan ordered. Her shoulder is fine."

She dropped the chart back on the bed and went to pull back the curtain. Vanessa, dropping Edwina's hand, blocked her way.

"Excuse me, but she most definitely does not have dementia. She is dying from cancer, an effect of which is constant urinary tract infections. She cannot tolerate a suprapubic catheter and her consultant changed her last week from long term Trimethoprim to prophylactic Nitrofurantoin, so we all know her confusion is linked to the infections."

By throwing in the drug names and some terminology, Vanessa hoped the doctor would respond with a more considered approach.

Looking at Vanessa, she spoke slowly and deliberately.

"I don't know anything about that, but she clearly has dementia and a CT scan will rule out any additional brain injury from the fall."

As an aside she added, "And no one dies from bladder cancer."

Holding the other woman's gaze, Vanessa said very plainly, "Then I suggest you find her urology notes and get a registrar down here now to speak to you about her ongoing treatment. Mr Edwards made it very clear that should she be brought in to A&E, his team must be contacted."

Without further discussion, the doctor left, with the nurse still hovering near the end of the bed.

"You OK, love?" She said to Vanessa, who couldn't quite believe what she had just heard and was breathing heavily, trying to keep the frustration out of her voice.

"No, I'm not. I want the urology team involved now and I don't want that woman near our mother again."

She was seething and was struggling hard not to cry, feeling that everything they were trying to do was being blocked by bureaucracy and incompetence.

The nurse laid a calming hand on her arm. "I'll sort it."

Turning to Edwina, she said, "Now, my love, how about a cold drink?"

Chapter 32

Dan pulled up outside Sunset House and removed his sunglasses. As always, he steeled himself to be ready to face the nursing home and his mother-in-law. He envied Michael's ability to chat about inconsequential things with her and his brother-in-law seemed oblivious to the smell that always now emanated from both her and her surroundings.

Vanessa got out of the car, picking up the small arrangement of golden roses and freesias that had been sitting on the back seat. Today marked the 70th anniversary of Edwina and James' wedding and both daughters always provided a floral contribution including the yellow roses that had made up Edwina's bridal bouquet.

She had expected to be visiting alone, but Dan had offered to keep her company. He hadn't seen Edwina since the fractious meeting with Jennifer in the spring. A combination of heavy workload and Vanessa's knowledge that he didn't enjoy visiting, meant he had managed to avoid any trips to Sunset House for the last three months. Caitlin had kept her mother company sometimes and Ross and Charlotte had made intermittent trips at weekends.

This morning though, Dan felt he couldn't put it off any longer and had suggested that maybe they go out for a pub lunch on their way back. Diana and Michael had friends staying for the weekend, so they were taking some time off. Dan saw it as an obligation to support his wife today.

The curtains to Edwina's room were closed as they rang the entry bell at the front door.

"She must be resting," Vanessa said, signing the visitor book and scanning the names above it as she always did, to check if Jennifer's name appeared.

Standing in the doorway, her room was in semi darkness but Edwina could clearly be seen sitting in her armchair, mouth ajar and head resting against the wing back sides. "Jesus, she looks awful," Dan exclaimed from the doorway, rather louder than he'd intended. Vanessa looked sharply at him, not in anger but his response was telling. Seeing Edwina every couple of days, it was difficult to mark her deterioration but Dan, not having laid eyes on her in the last few weeks, had given a genuine shocked reaction, which indicated just how much her mother had gone downhill.

"I'm so sorry," Dan whispered. "But she's lost so much weight."

Edwina had been a tall, lithe woman in her youth but Dan and indeed Vanessa, had only ever known her as relatively solid. You wouldn't say she was overweight, but neither was she waif like. Now, she seemed to Dan to have almost folded in on herself. Her once proud posture was more stooped and her chest seemed to be concave, as if every breath was an effort. Her wedding ring was half-way up her knuckle, where it used to be firmly wedged at the base of her finger, sometimes leaving a ridge mark in the skin on her lower digit. Her hair was thin and wispy and reminded him of pictures of wizened hags around the fire in MacBeth.

Vanessa moved into the room, indicating to Dan that he should take a seat on the bed. He marvelled at his wife's ability to take it all in her stride as she placed the flowers on the table in front of Edwina and busied herself tidying the papers and magazines and folding her mother's nightdress, which was on the chair back, tucking it tidily under the pillow on her bed. He realised, with some shame, that this was what Vanessa was dealing with on a daily basis and he hadn't appreciated how difficult it must be for her.

The smell in the room was overpowering—a strong combination of bleach mixed with the unmistakable aroma of ammonia. The commode sat at the end of the room, like some throne, waiting to brought forward and used by its owner.

Since her discharge from A&E a couple of weeks ago, Edwina had been having additional nursing for the skin excoriation caused by the constant leaking of urine. The urology team, who had eventually been called by the emergency department team, had been kind and thorough. Edwina had been lucid enough to complain about the constant itching and burning she was experiencing and examination had revealed red raw skin, stretching from her groin and surrounding her vaginal area, spreading to her buttocks. She must have been in an agony of discomfort that she was either too embarrassed or too ashamed to mention to the nursing staff or her daughters. Both Vanessa and Diana had been horrified to know just how her skin had deteriorated. They'd naively assumed that the nurses would have raised it with the local doctor and provided her with relief, but it had come to light that Edwina was refusing any help with hygiene, adamant she could cope. Since she had returned to Sunset House however, the fight appeared to have left her and she submitted quietly to the daily ritual of antiseptic washes and emollient creams to help her raw and blistered skin. The urology registrar had explained it wasn't unusual at this stage of the disease and likely the size of the tumour was now causing both bladder and bowel control issues.

"It's a question of keeping her comfortable," was the line being taken by the professionals.

Dan and Vanessa chatted for a while about day-to-day things, the business and children and where they would stop for lunch on the way home.

Edwina stirred.

Gently stroking her mother's hand, so she wouldn't be surprised as she came to, Vanessa waited for consciousness to reach her mother. Edwina's eyes opened and she stared at her youngest daughter.

"Hello you, you've had a nice sleep."

"Hello, darling, how long have you been here?" Edwina's voice was croaky and reedy from lack of use.

"Not long," though in truth, they'd been sat here for the best part of an hour.

"Hello, mother." Dan leaned forward so that his face was in her peripheral vision. He was hoping he wouldn't have to kiss her a greeting. The longer he had watched her, the more the impression of a living cadaver had been on his mind.

"Hello, Dan." Edwina sat a little straighter and appeared to make a bit more of an effort on realising she had a proper visitor. However, the effort of movement seemed to exhaust her and she slumped against the chair side.

"You look a bit uncomfortable there," Vanessa said, reaching across and picking up a couple of plump but soft cushions.

"Let's give you some padding," and she gently pulled her mother forward, whilst tucking the cushions around her. Easing Edwina backwards, her mother smiled her thanks and Vanessa noticed how thin she had become, fragile bones in her wrists and legs. Her once 'chunky' calves—always a bane of Edwina's life—now resembled bird's limbs with little hiding the protruding bones and the discoloured skin indicating poor circulation.

Vanessa showed her the flowers and Edwina declared she was delighted with them.

"Oh, you've got visitors!" Brenda, their favourite care assistant, was passing by with a tea trolley.

"Would you like a cuppa and a biscuit, Edwina?"

Edwina smiled her thanks and shook her head.

"Go on, lovely, I've a bourbon here with your name on it."

"No, thank you, dear, I'm fine."

Gesturing to the pot, Brenda asked Dan and Vanessa if they'd like any. Vanessa declined but Dan said yes and getting up, he went to the doorway to receive the regulation green cup and saucer.

"Ooo, you're a big lad," Brenda observed, looking up at his 6'2" frame from her 5'2" perch. "You'll need three biccies," and winking at him, passed the tea over.

Laughing, he took the proffered cup and biscuits and went back to sit on the bed.

"I'll be back shortly with your lunch," Brenda informed them as she set off, tea trolley rattling along the carpeted hallway.

"What's for lunch today?" Vanessa enquired.

"No idea. I'm not really hungry."

Edwina closed her eyes again.

"So, what have you been up to?" She said, keeping her lids closed and her head tilted towards the sunlight, in what reminded her daughter of a sunbathing pose.

They talked about nothing in particular, Dan asking her about the snooker that was on the television and the plans for their August holiday. But Edwina was clearly exhausted. "Well, we must let you get ready for lunch," Vanessa declared picking up her bag and sunglasses.

"Happy Anniversary, Mummy," she said quietly, kissing Edwina on the forehead.

"Thank you, darling, and thank you for the lovely flowers. It was good to see you, Dan, don't go working too hard."

Digging deep, Dan bent and kissed his mother-in-law's cheek. She smiled up at him and patted his hand.

Waving from the doorway, Vanessa blew her mother a kiss and they signed themselves out of Sunset and went towards their car. Looking in at her windows as they passed, Edwina's eyes were once again closed.

Chapter 33

"Shall we stop for a coffee?"

Diana stood in the hallway of the bungalow—a slight sheen on her brow and her hair slipping from the messy bun, tendrils sticking to her damp forehead. The sisters had worked solidly for a couple of hours, beginning the process of clearing the bungalow.

When it became evident that Edwina would not be returning home, they'd had the difficult conversation about starting to sort through all her things. They had agreed early in her illness that all the time she could visit and there'd been the slightest chance she could return home, everything had been kept as she'd left it. But it was now nearly six months since her last visit and as she was growing weaker by the day, she rarely left her bed, never mind her room at Sunset House. They'd come to accept that she wouldn't be returning home.

Whilst both Vanessa and Diana had reservations about doing this whilst Edwina was still alive, they knew it would be a big job and it gave them something to focus on and the practicalities of the task distracted them from the inevitable outcome. It had been their home for over 40 years, so they'd agreed to make a start on going through cupboards and sideboards, wardrobes and dressing tables, to make a dent in the chore.

Already today, Vanessa had uncovered some cookery and housekeeping magazines from the 1950s and Diana had unearthed a tiny dance card from a church event in 1938 that both Edwina and James had attended as teenagers. They kept getting distracted by these small reminders of their parents' lives, but found it comforting too. Every Christmas and birthday card their father had sent to his wife—sometimes from far flung parts of the world—had been carefully stored in boxes and safely kept under spare beds and on top cupboards.

Other, less sentimental items they were moving into the garage, ready for the skip to take away the detritus of a 1970s bungalow. Plastic artificial flowers, rattan waste bins that had loose threads and holes, bath mats, pots of paint, the ironing board and broken flower pots were gradually being stacked up. Dan and Michael had offered to help with the task and the sisters had said they'd appreciate their muscle and hefting skills once the skip was on site. They had declared this would not be until after Edwina had gone, when they would look at getting an antique dealer to come and value the house contents.

At her enquiry about the coffee, Vanessa looked up from her position on the floor. She'd been sorting through her mother's clothes and shoes. Recognising that Edwina would never wear her wardrobes of clothes again, they were making piles to take to the charity shops. She would appreciate people being able to make good use of any items.

Two piece knitted suits were folded on the bed, stacked alongside jumpers, cardigans and evening dresses from long ago dinner dances and ship launch parties. A beautiful dress and coat in gold satin, with pearl encrusted decoration, hung from one of the wardrobe doors. The one-off designer outfit had been Edwina's choice for Jennifer's wedding. She had never parted with it though it had never been worn again.

"Sounds like a good idea. I bought a couple of cakes with me—let's break those out. I think we've earned them."

Whilst the kettle boiled, they decided to move the exercise bike into the garage. Edwina had bought it after her first hip replacement operation to ensure she got some exercise and whilst it had been used intermittently (mainly by the grandchildren for a laugh), it had been gathering dust in the front room that she used as a study, for a number of years.

It was surprisingly heavy and the two women lugged it to the front door, struggling to manoeuvre it outside. As they manhandled it up the garden path, both puffing with the effort, Diana muttered, "I bet this is the most exercise anyone's ever had from this bloody thing!" Vanessa stopped, collapsing with laughter at her sister's comment.

"Well, bloody thing should have gone years ago."

Once the offending bike was in the garage, they took themselves off with their coffee and cakes into the garden. It was in full summer bloom, shrubs covered in blowsy florals, sagging a little in the heat and the fir trees lining the edges of the half acre property, provided a cool green palette for them to stop and rest.

"Hellooooo."

They heard the side gate close and saw Edith coming round the corner. She reminded Vanessa of a nervous sparrow, hopping along, waiting to be pounced on by the local cat. She reminded Diana of a nosy old witch!

"Thought I'd see how Mum's doing? What news? How is she? Have they said if she can come home?"

Tilting her head to one side, she finally paused for breath and looked enquiringly at the sisters.

Sensing a rising ire in Diana, Vanessa took the lead.

"She's not great. She's struggling now and doesn't want visitors."

This last part, whilst true, was also for the benefit of stopping the inevitable request she knew Edith would voice.

"We're going over in a bit to see her. It's a difficult day. It's 25 years since daddy died and we always spend it with her—not that she's likely to know much about it this year."

"Never mind, it won't matter to her," Edith said with her usual lack of tact.

"But it does to us!" Diana retorted caustically.

"Of course," Edith had the good grace to look a little embarrassed. "So, if you'll forgive us," Diana stood in an effort to end the conversation.

"And Jennifer?"

"What about Jennifer?"

"Does she know—about Edwina I mean?"

"I doubt it. Jennifer hasn't shown her face for months now—not since she learned there's nothing of value here and she's not an elected advocate for Mummy."

"It's just she'd probably like the opportunity to say goodbye," Edith persisted. "Do you think you best contact her?"

"Jennifer is not our concern—and anyway, we have no means to contact her," Vanessa said becoming irritated.

"She needs to understand the consequences of her actions. Turning up only when you feel like it doesn't mean you get what you want when it suits you. Mummy is adamant she doesn't want to see her so we must respect her wishes."

"People often change their minds towards the end," Edith continued. "You'd hate her to go to her grave with regrets."

Vanessa recognised the flash of anger in her sister's eyes and saw and heard their mother's voice in Diana's clipped response.

"Our mother has nothing to be regretful for. Now, if you'll excuse us, we have things to do. Goodbye, Edith," and she walked across the grass and into the house via the back door. "Bye, thanks for calling," Vanessa said. She felt a little embarrassed by Diana's abruptness. She followed her sister into the house, shutting the door behind her, so Edith would get the message that there was nothing more to be said.

Putting her mug in the sink, she heard sobbing coming from the bathroom down the hallway and found Diana on the edge of the primrose bath tub, uncontrollably wracked with tears.

Saying nothing, she knelt down, wrapped her arms around her sister and felt her own hot tears course down her face.

"God, I hate that woman," Diana said as the wave of emotion began to subside. "I don't hate many people but I just look at her and my back goes up."

"No shit, Sherlock!"

Diana smiled between her tears. "It's all a bit shit isn't it?"

"Yep, but hey, we always knew it was going to be. At least we're here together and we'll get through it."

"Come on, let's pack up for today and head off to Eastbourne. I'd like to stop at the crematorium on the way and drop some flowers off for daddy."

Washing up their mugs and making sure the house was secure, they went out to the drive. The new neighbours were cleaning their car and Maureen, who they'd only met a couple of times, headed their way.

"How's Mum?"

"Not great, we're off there now," Vanessa said, putting her bag on the back seat and pulling her sunglasses down from the top of her head.

"Only, we were wondering how long the house is likely to be empty. It's very quiet and obviously no one's been here for some time now."

Whilst Vanessa resisted the urge to ask if their 93-year-old mother had had many raves prior to her hospitalisation, Diana said, ever so sweetly.

"Don't worry, she'll be dead soon and then we can sell it to some party animals. We'll pass on your good wishes to her," and with that, she got in the driver's side of the car and slammed the door.

Vanessa gave a weak smile at Maureen, who had the good grace to look ashamed at her question, and she settled herself into the passenger seat.

"For fuck's sake, what's wrong with these people!" Diana exclaimed. She wasn't given to bad language, so Vanessa knew she'd been pushed to her limit.

"Oh, I think they've all got the message," and giving a rueful laugh, they pulled away from the close and headed east.

Chapter 34

The room was in darkness. A little evening light penetrated the curtains but Edwina's bed was too far up the room for it to make any impact. She'd lost track of time, failing to know whether it was morning or night. Every minute of every day was taken up by the pains in her joints. The very marrow of her bones felt like they were on fire and despite the efforts of all the various nurses, she just couldn't get comfortable.

The afternoon had been punctuated by a visit from Diana and Vanessa. They'd brought her jelly, trying to encourage her to eat something. Her appetite had abandoned her some time ago and everything they tried to get her to eat tasted bitter and caused her to gag. She'd forced a teaspoon of jelly down but it came back, violently.

The heatwave of a few weeks ago had returned and the girls had kindly brought her some lavender water to place on her brow. It cooled her forehead and the smell reminded her of her mother. It was a pleasant aroma and a break from the constant smell of sickness and impending death that she knew was emanating from her every pore.

Diana had gently brushed Edwina's hair whilst they chatted quietly together. Vanessa rubbed her mother's hands with some cream, trying to replenish some moisture into the cracked skin.

Edwina had drifted in and out of the conversation, but was content to have the distraction from her pains for a while. At one point, she'd been aware they were both quietly crying. She didn't like them upset. It was her job to protect them—but she was just so tired.

Now, some hours later, she lay in the semi darkness listening to the sounds of the nurses and care assistants moving from room to room, preparing the residents for their night-time rituals. The medicine trolley, with its one squeaky wheel, limped along the corridor, announcing its arrival to everyone with the promise of painkillers and medications to usher them through another night.

Edwina became aware of a movement at the far side of her room. In the half-light she couldn't distinguish who it was. Nurse? Care Assistant? Intruder?

Whoever it was appeared to be going through Edwina's chest of drawers. Outside in the corridor, a light came on throwing a beam of brightness through the doorway and lighting up the profile of the unknown visitor. Jennifer.

She was engrossed in her task. Carefully moving blouses, nightdresses and cardigans, all the time sweeping her hand through the layers. Whether she was looking for money or jewellery, Edwina wasn't sure but she knew her eldest daughter was up to no good.

"Not sure my knickers will fit you!"

Edwina's voice was a lot more forceful and sarcastic than she thought she was capable of any longer.

The younger woman spun around, removing her hands from the drawer and closing it behind her back.

"Hello. I was just putting away some of your washing whilst you had a rest. We don't want stuff lying around and you were sound."

Edwina eyed her firstborn. This golden child who had brought a different kind of love and joy to James and Edwina's world had devastated them with her lies, deceit and troublemaking. For so many years, they'd made excuses for her, talked themselves into believing she'd had numerous reasons for doing what she did. Edwina well remembered James' utter despair just before he died. He held himself responsible for all the pain and anguish Jennifer had caused, but towards the end, he had also accepted that she was a grown woman who had to take responsibility for her actions. He had been adamant she wasn't to attend his funeral and despite Edwina trying in the intervening years since to forgive her daughter, Jennifer continued to wreak havoc wherever she went. The charity collapse and fraud case of a few years previously was the straw that broke the camel's back and still weighed heavily on Edwina. How could her child be so callous and demonstrate such a lack of morals?

So, as she now looked at the woman before her, Edwina's heart hardened and her eyes narrowed.

"I think we both know you're talking rubbish. I've little enough time left to spend it on your lies. I presume it's money or at least something of value that you're after?"

Jennifer's eyes widened as if the mere thought shocked her. "Mummy, I…"

"Save it, Jennifer. You're acting skills are up to your usual high standards but I've had enough. I'm lying in this god forsaken room, waiting to die, unable to enjoy any small pleasures any more. I can't read, I can't move and I'm surrounded by well-intentioned staff who seem to think some cheerful banter will improve my situation. You, my girl, are a thief and a liar. I have very few regrets but you are most definitely my greatest. I regret every day that I excused your behaviour and I can only ask forgiveness of all those you've cheated and lied to. And top of that list is your sisters. They've been rocks through all the decades of your misdemeanours. I've made excuse after excuse for you and bless them, they've never said I was a stupid old woman, though no doubt they thought it. Well, let me make it clear, lady—there is nothing for you. Your part of the inheritance was swallowed up years ago! The mortgage payments, the county court judgements, debt payments to foreign businesses so you could leave their country, not to mention the failed businesses I've invested in for you and the bail monies. It's all gone, Jennifer—you've had your lot. Everything that is left is to be divided between your sisters and there's documentary evidence accompanying my Will going back forty years, so you can forget about challenging it. I've made sure no lawyer would take on the case—you bled us dry."

Whilst she'd been talking, Edwina had been fiddling with her eternity ring. Solid gold with oak leaves that stood out in relief across the width of the band, James had given it to her in 1968 on their twenty-first wedding anniversary with the sentiment that if he could, he'd marry her all over again. Edwina was not short of jewelled rings, but this one held a special place in her heart and was a 'keeper' for her wedding ring, always worn and always treasured.

Removing it from her bony fingers was easy today, where it used to be a tussle to extricate it if she was gardening or cooking. Now, it slipped smoothly over her knuckle and into her palm. Giving it a final rub between her fingers she threw it across the room at Jennifer.

"Here, it's all I have left. Take it, pawn it, melt it down. Do whatever you want with it. You've had your pound of flesh and then some. Now go."

And with that, Edwina closed her eyes and sank back against the pillows, breathing heavily with the exhaustion of her speech, but feeling remarkably calm and content.

Jennifer fell to the floor, scrabbling around in the darkness under the bed in an effort to locate the ring. It was probably worth a couple of thousand and certainly wasn't the first piece of her mother's jewellery she'd have sold. She wasn't surprised about the Will but the information it was legally watertight to any challenge was unexpected. Still, she was nothing if not resourceful and had already made inroads into finding a role as an office manager at a local charity. Of course, she'd used a different name to avoid any police checks and her story about being abroad for the last few years nursing a dying parent ensured she'd easily covered off the questions about her lack of employment in recent times. She'd soon be set up with an income and the cash from the ring would keep her going for a while.

Her hand made contact with the metal and she picked it up, popping it directly into her pocket. Looking at her mother, she realised this would be the last time she'd see her. She'd never again have to account for her actions to this matriarch. There was a tiny part of her conscience that also registered that there wouldn't be anyone to fight her corner or bail her out when needed, but in true Jennifer style, she'd worry about that when the time came.

When Edwina opened her eyes, she was alone. Jennifer had gone and Edwina knew it was the last time she'd see her daughter. Sighing, she mentally ticked off this final task. She'd protected Diana and Vanessa as much as she could. Now, she waited for the inevitable ending.

Chapter 35

Vanessa tossed the throw cushions off the bed and peeled back the duvet. It was another warm night and the combination of sticky air and raging menopausal hormones meant that most nights she slept fitfully, one minute hot enough to fry an egg on her thigh and next, almost shivering with the cooling breeze.

She heard Dan's electric toothbrush stop and he emerged from the en-suite. Long days on site project managing the new development meant his arms were a chestnut brown, as was his neck and face. She noticed his hair thinning on top and the exposed skin also had a nutty brown tinge. The work kept him fit and he enjoyed being outside, filling his days with practical tasks. The office admin bored him though in the last six months he'd had to take up the slack as Vanessa had pushed much of the day-to-day stuff onto him, allowing her to spend time with her mother.

Realising she'd taken him for granted, Vanessa thought she ought to arrange a break for them in the next couple of months. They'd planned an August holiday over twelve months ago, but with Edwina failing and as they were fast approaching the end of July, they'd agreed to postpone the trip.

She climbed into bed, pushing Simba towards the bottom of the mattress. The Labrador looked pained at her rejection of his warm fur coat heating her side of the bed, but he soon resettled himself and began gently snoring.

"Are you reading?" She looked at Dan. Some nights, he was too exhausted from work to do anything but collapse, sleeping soundly as soon as his head hit the pillow.

"Yeah for a bit. You?"

She nodded, picking up her reading glasses and removing her bookmark from the historical novel she'd started months ago.

She'd not been to Sunset House today. After a solid four days sitting with Edwina, Diana had suggested she take a day off. Her sister had phoned earlier to say she'd popped in but Edwina was exhausted. They'd swapped her bed for some other special mattress allowing them to turn her more easily but the effort of moving had been draining. Having eaten nothing for days and struggling now to keep down water, her daughters had been wetting her chapped lips with small sponges dipped in sugared water. She hadn't really been conscious of this kindness and any movement now seemed to induce a feeling of sickness. The lack of nourishment meant she spent much of her time wracked with the effort of dry heaving and both Vanessa and Diana had found this difficult to watch.

"If she was a dog, she'd have been put down by now," Diana had wailed as they'd sat in Vanessa's car the previous day.

"Where's the dignity in this?"

"I know but she doesn't really seem to be aware, so it's probably worse for us than her. She must be near the end now."

The professionals had been saying for over a week now that 'it's likely to be today' but still Edwina held on.

Vanessa realised she'd read the same sentence four or five times and it still hadn't registered.

"I'm calling it a night," she told Dan, putting her book and glasses on the bedside table.

"Night, sleep well. I won't be long."

"Ok, sleep tight, love you."

She kissed him and turned over getting comfortable despite Simba having slinked his way back up towards the top of the bed. She heard Dan sigh. He really didn't like the dog on the bed but now wasn't the time to mention it.

A few minutes later, his light went off and she felt him lie down, his arm draped over her. He was soon breathing rhythmically.

Then the phone rang.

Jumping up and putting her bedside light back on, she saw the caller ID said, 'Di.' The clock said 11:10 pm.

"Hi."

"Hi, Sunset have just phoned. Mummy's gone downhill a lot in the last hour or so; they think it will be tonight. Do you want to go?"

They had discussed at length whether, if the need arose, they'd go and be with Edwina at the end. They both felt they wanted to hold her hands as she went on her final journey but they were also very aware that Edwina would hate it. They had argued with her when James was dying and whilst both women had wanted to be with their father, Edwina was adamant he would not want them there. In the end, the hospital had phoned in the early hours to say he'd gone quietly when a nurse was with him. Secretly, both Diana and Vanessa were sure Edwina had instructed them not to ring until it was too late, but neither had been brave enough to ever actually confront their mother.

So, now they were faced with the same dilemma. Do what would be comforting to them, or respect their mother's wishes and let her leave alone. Vanessa bit her nail.

"I really would like to be with her."

Dan was watching her, poised to get up and take his wife if needed.

"But she'd hate it, wouldn't she?"

Vanessa realised she was being unfair, asking her sister to validate the decision.

"No, I think you're right and Sunset knew, though they wanted us to be aware. They'll call me and I'll let you know as soon as I hear anything."

"Ok, speak later."

Vanessa put the phone down and Dan looked enquiringly at her.

"She's gone downhill, they think it'll be tonight."

"Do you want to go?"

"Yes and no. Di agrees we shouldn't. She's going to ring as soon as she hears."

Climbing back into bed, she was enveloped in Dan's arms, resting her face against his bare chest. He stroked her hair whilst she silently cried and Simba curled himself into the crook of her legs, adding his own comfort.

"Do you want a cuppa?" Dan asked when the weeping subsided.

"No, you're ok. Let's try and get some rest."

They lay down in each other's arms and Dan was soon sleeping. She smiled wryly, knowing he'd try to stay awake but he was exhausted from the day's exertions and he couldn't evade sleep any longer.

She lay awake in the darkness, going over the last few months in her mind. The temptation to drag on some clothes and dash down to the coast was almost overwhelming. But then the image of her mother's face came to mind and knowing how much Edwina would disapprove of her lack of resolve, she stayed where she was.

After a while, she looked at the clock. Three a.m.

Light was peeking through the shutters as a July morning was breaking. As quietly as she could, Vanessa slid from the bed. Dan stirred but stayed sleeping. She put on a light cardigan over her summer pyjamas and pulling the bedroom door closed behind her, went downstairs, turning off the night alarm before opening the kitchen door. Simba had slid off the bed, following her in the hope of snacks or at least some milk in his bowl.

Chapter 36

She put the kettle on. Opening the back door, the dawn chorus greeted her. This was her favourite time of day in the summer. The heat of the day hadn't got going but there was a warmth and the early morning light was mellow, allowing your senses to appreciate the sun's rays without the harshness of a full summer glare.

Taking her tea, she strolled to the swing seat at the end of the garden. The soft green grass was lush and the lack of any morning dew meant she could easily walk the length of the lawn without the danger of her bare feet slipping. Simba followed her and after cocking his leg against the hydrangea bush, followed her to the seat, looking hopefully at her and waiting for the signal to be allowed to jump up and join her. Dan would have told him to bugger off but he knew the doleful brown eyes were irresistible to his mistress. Smiling at him, Vanessa clicked her tongue and up he went settling himself alongside her. Absently, she patted his head and stroked the silky ears.

"Good lad."

This was such an odd time—almost like the eye of the storm. Quiet, calm and silent after the hurly burly of the last six months and before the hustle and bustle of funeral arrangements, house sale and of course, the waves of grief she knew would accompany the death of her mother.

Vanessa didn't know how long she sat there. Watching the garden gradually coming to life, seeing the pots of flowers, their heads turning towards the warming sun, and watching the birds emerging and having their morning snack from the range of feeders dotted around the bushes. The odd car could be heard going up the road, indicating that the day had started for the early commuters.

Her tea had sat in her hands, undrunk and now cold. She thought she best move and get an early shower, then she could legitimately leave and get to Sunset House before Edwina died.

Standing up, she heard a noise. Unsure what or where it was coming from, she looked up over the neighbouring rooftops.

Dancing through the morning light were, what appeared to be thousands of birds. Their balletic movement was mesmerising, swirling, dipping and swooping in time to some unheard music. Vanessa knew that these avian sights took place at sunset and usually in the autumn and winter months, so was transfixed by their appearance. In the quiet of the July morning, their whiling pirouette with the whispering rustle of their wings was magnetic and majestic. The murmuration soared towards the heavens and disappeared over the horizon.

Her fascination at their display was interrupted by the harsh tone of the ringing telephone.

Chapter 37

The family gathered at Edwina's bungalow, waiting for the hearse to arrive.

Mark and Ruth had arrived from New York the previous weekend and now sat on the sofa in Edwina's living room, with Caitlin, Ross, Sam and Charlotte. The siblings and their cousins chatted quietly. Vanessa kept an eye on Caitlin who had been particularly quiet all day. Knowing Edwina's end was near hadn't made it any easier and now being here, in her grandmother's home but without her sitting in her usual chair in the corner of the lounge felt strange and somewhat disloyal.

As with everything in her life, Edwina had planned and paid for her funeral. Both Vanessa and Diana had put together a service they felt reflected their mother perfectly. Hymns—no modern music—and a male vicar who would reflect on her life without unnecessary displays of emotion. No one standing up and making speeches. There were family flowers only, with a request, as per Edwina's instructions, for donations to the RNLI.

They'd agreed the hearse would leave from her home. Edwina had always sworn she'd only leave 'feet first' and whilst she hadn't technically been able to do so, her daughters felt it was right to give her that opportunity now. As befitted their mother's sense of tradition, they both wore mourning outfits with hats and gloves. Trying to find black dresses and hats in the middle of summer was a challenge but one they'd risen to and now standing together in their family home, surrounded by James and Edwina's things, they felt a sense of pride and resolve in honouring their parents' memories.

"They're here," Michael announced. He and Dan had been chatting in the hallway, waiting for the cars to arrive.

The children made their way down towards the front door with Mark stopping in the room that Edwina had used as a study at the front of the house. The old ship's bell that had belonged to James, which Edwina had bequeathed to Mark as he'd love to ring it as a little boy, hung on the study wall. He'd asked his mother and aunt if he could toll the bell when his grandmother arrived back at the house as a sailors' tribute and both had tearfully agreed she would have been delighted.

Now, as the bell tolled its final mournful farewell, Vanessa gripped Diana's hand hard. They'd been through so much these last few months; the frustrations, tears, laughter and strain had been a shared experience that neither would ever forget.

Having tolled eight bells, Mark exited the house walking to the car that would transport the youngsters to the crematorium. Dan and Michael settled themselves in the first car and locking up the house, Diana and Vanessa walked the pathway towards the hearse. Both immaculately dressed, the undertaker, who had known the family for years, smiled. "She'd be very proud of you both. You look stunning."

Smiling their thanks but not trusting themselves to speak, they got into the back of the limousine and breathing deeply, holding hands, they went to say their goodbyes to Edwina.

Chapter 38

Sitting in the evening light, Vanessa had kicked off her shoes. The funeral had gone smoothly and the wake had been a celebration of Edwina's life. For an old lady, the turnout had been spectacular and there were many stories of Edwina's kindness to people over the years.

The venue had overlooked the Cuckmere Valley—beloved of James and Edwina, both from their honeymoon, to their family life, dog walks and summer sunsets. It had seemed the perfect location to say their farewells and now, sat in Diana and Michael's garden, wine in hand, Vanessa felt something like relief for the first time in months.

The men were chatting quietly and the young adults had all gone to the Indian for a meal together, leaving the oldies to catch their breath after a long and tiring day.

"At least Jennifer didn't show," Vanessa said, swirling the merlot in her glass.

It had been a concern that their eldest sister would make an appearance and cause a scene. Fortunately, against all the odds, she'd stayed away and they both realised that now, they'd never have to see her again.

"If you ignore Jennifer, technically I'm the oldest in the family now," Diana mused. "The matriarch!" her sister laughed.

"Thanks so much! God, it makes me feel old when you realise you are now the oldies in the family. Comes to us all, I suppose."

Dan and Michael sipped their beers. Their wives had aged over the last half year, but tonight, they could see the strain beginning to ebb away.

"A toast," Dan said, "to mother."

Raising their glasses and clinking them together as the sun began to set, they said with cheerfulness and hope, "To Mummy."

Epilogue

Vanessa stood beneath the sold board. It was now six months since Edwina had died and finally the house sale had gone through. It had taken less time to clear it than both the sisters had thought and today was the day that they handed the keys to the estate agent. The buyers were a family with young children, dogs, cats, rabbits and apparently a chinchilla.

When they'd had the prospective offer put in and learned about the buyers, Diana had chuckled.

"That'll liven things up around here. The neighbours said they didn't like it so quiet."

"I'm not sure they meant they wanted kids running around," her sister retorted and they'd laughed. Both had agreed that James and Edwina would be thrilled to know a family were going to be making new memories in their precious home rather than a staid, retired couple and their father would certainly have found it highly amusing that perhaps the neighbours were getting more than they'd bargained for.

Having dropped the keys off at the agents and said their goodbyes, Diana suggested a walk by the beach. The January day was chilly but both were wrapped up and there was a clear blue sky and freshness to the air that both cleared the head and made your teeth ache.

They set off towards the seafront, stopping in the High Street to get a takeaway coffee and slice of cake. Making their way to the end of the promenade, they headed for the benches. A few months before Diana had heard that the Town Council were placing some benches, specially designed to resemble a shoal of fishes, so it looked like they were heading out to sea. You could buy a little fish plaque to have placed on the bench with hundreds of others. Edwina had requested her ashes be scattered on the same rose bed as James' so they had no formal headstone to remember her by. Diana and Vanessa had thought a little fish, heading out to sea in remembrance of their mother was ideal and the installation was now finished and open to the public.

Sitting together in the winter sun, sipping their coffees and admiring the blue, steel grey water there rose a wave of birds from the chalk cliffs. Something had startled them and as one they flew out towards the horizon, away from danger.

"The morning Mummy died, there was a murmuration of birds over the house," Vanessa said to her sister.

"It was strange—wrong time of the year and wrong time of the day but must have been around the time she died. I know it sounds weird, but I find that rather comforting."

"We had the same," Diana said, startled that her sister had experienced the same phenomenon.

"Michael thought I was nuts when I saw it, but he came out and realised it wasn't my imagination."

"Maybe her way of telling us she was leaving. Mind you, I didn't tell Dan—he'd have thought I was just being superstitious."

The sisters sat together, both quiet, lost in their own thoughts but content in each other's company. Finishing their coffee, they stood up and, saying goodbye to their mother's little engraved silver fish, linked arms and headed for home.